mothers and dogs

ALSO BY FABIO MORÁBITO

Home Reading Service

mothers

AND

dogs

STORIES

FABIO MORÁBITO

Translated from the Spanish by Curtis Bauer

OTHER PRESS • NEW YORK

Originally published in Spanish as *Madres y perros* in 2016
by Sexto Piso, Mexico City
Copyright © 2016 Fabio Morábito
Translation rights arranged by Agencia Literaria CBQ SL
www.agencialiterariacbq.com
Translation copyright © 2023 Curtis Bauer

Production editor: Yvonne E. Cárdenas
Text designer: Jennifer Daddio
This book was set in Gotham Rounded and Cochin
by Alpha Design & Composition of Pittsfield, NH

1 3 5 7 9 10 8 6 4 2

Library of Congress Cataloging-in-Publication Data
Names: Morábito, Fabio, 1955- author. | Bauer, Curtis, 1970- translator.
Title: Mothers and dogs : stories / Fabio Morábito ; translated
from the Spanish by Curtis Bauer.
Other titles: Madres y perros. English
Description: New York : Other Press, [2023] | Originally published in Spanish
as Madres y perros in 2016 by Sexto Piso, Mexico City.
Identifiers: LCCN 2022027410 (print) | LCCN 2022027411 (ebook) |
ISBN 9781635420821 (paperback) | ISBN 9781635420838 (ebook)
Subjects: LCSH: Morábito, Fabio, 1955-—Translations into English. |
LCGFT: Short stories.
Classification: LCC PQ7298.23.O724 M3413 2023 (print) |
LCC PQ7298.23.O724 (ebook) | DDC 863/.64—dc23/eng/20220614
LC record available at https://lccn.loc.gov/2022027410
LC ebook record available at https://lccn.loc.gov/2022027411

contents

the sailboat

The "For Sale" sign was hanging in the window of the room he had shared with his brother. Ricaño pulled a piece of paper out of his jacket pocket so he could write down the number of the real estate agency and then took a few steps back to contemplate the five-story building where he was born. Compared to the new buildings on the street, it looked conspicuously outdated. He crossed to the other sidewalk to go into a café, which had been a greengrocer's when he was a kid, and walked directly to the phone. He dialed the number he had just written down and a woman's voice answered. Ricaño said that he was interested in seeing the apartment that was for sale and the woman gave him a brief description of the place before telling him the price. He confirmed that he wanted to see it and the other warned him: "The tenants are still there. I mention this because some people don't like to see an apartment with people inside." Ricaño told her it was better that way, that it would give him a better idea of the space because it was furnished. The woman said she would call the tenants right away to notify them of his visit and they made a plan to meet at the entrance to the building at four that afternoon. She asked his name and he replied "Santibáñez."

After hanging up he ordered a cup of coffee at the bar. He gave himself twenty minutes. He imagined that was enough time for the women from the agency to call the tenants, notifying them about his visit that afternoon. He ordered a second coffee and glanced at the sports paper someone had left on a table. He looked at his watch, paid, and crossed the street. He rang the intercom doorbell and a young girl answered. He said he was the person interested in buying the apartment. The device crackled and a few seconds later a woman's voice asked him who he was.

"I'm Señor Santibáñez, the person interested in buying the apartment," Ricaño repeated.

"Weren't you supposed to come this afternoon?"

"Yes, but since I'm in the area it'd be more convenient for me to see it now, if it's not a bother."

The woman told him to wait a moment, and he heard the raspy noise a hand makes covering the intercom handle. He pressed his face against the glass to look inside the building and saw that everything was still the same: A strip of linoleum crossed the lobby leading to the elevator and stairs. A few minutes passed and he was about to ring the bell again, when he saw a girl approaching from the far end of the hallway. The girl observed Ricaño through the glass and opened the main door.

"Señor Santibáñez?" she asked.

"That's me."

She invited him in. As he followed her, he estimated that she was about sixteen years old. They climbed the five steps leading to the hallway with the first-floor apartments and the teen rapped her knuckles on the door three times. He read the last name on the small placard next to the doorbell: Del Valle. A woman in her forties opened the door; her features left no doubt that she was the girl's mother.

"Come in, and excuse the mess," she said without extending her hand.

3

"I'm the one who should apologize," Ricaño said, and standing in the entryway was enough for him to feel the traumatic certainty of having been a child within those walls. He was stunned by the sight of the lintels, the door handles, and, more than anything else, seeing the floor tiles again. He stood stock-still, and the woman, seeing he was self-conscious, said, "Come this way, please." But instead of following her, he squeezed the bridge of his nose to hide his emotions. She asked if he was feeling okay. "Excuse me," Ricaño said, covering his face with his hand. At that moment a girl, maybe four or five years old, appeared.

"Why's the man crying, Mamá?" she whispered.

Ricaño looked to the side so the girl couldn't see his face, turned around, and opened the door to leave, but it was latched with a chain lock; he tried to unlatch it and the teen came to help him, unfastened the chain, and opened the door. Ricaño walked out and stopped on the landing.

"Are you feeling ill, Señor Santibáñez?" the mother of the girls asked again. He took some tissues out of his jacket pocket and dried his eyes.

"Excuse me," he said. "This house brings back a lot of memories."

"You've been here before?"

4

"I lived here my whole childhood." He squeezed the bridge of his nose again and smiled weakly. "I've lived abroad for the last forty years. Whenever I come back, I come here. Three years ago I got up the nerve to ring the doorbell and an old man answered; I asked if I could come in but he refused. People have become distrustful these days. So when I saw the 'For Sale' sign I thought, this is the opportunity I've been waiting for."

"In other words, you're not interested in buying the apartment," the teen said.

"No, the truth is, I'm not. I just wanted to come in. Forgive me."

"He lied to us," the teen exclaimed, looking at her mother. Ricaño folded the tissues into his pocket and made a gesture to leave.

"Wait," the mother said. "Since you've already come in, look around if you want."

The teen, annoyed, took the little girl's hand, said "Come on!," went into one of the bedrooms with her, and slammed the door.

The woman looked at Ricaño. "This way, Señor Santibáñez."

"My name isn't Santibáñez," he said. "I gave the lady at the agency the name of a friend of mine, I don't know why. My name is Ricaño, look." He took out his wallet, removed his ID, and showed it to the woman, who looked at it and said, "Don't pay any attention to my daughter. You came on a bad day. Three months ago today my husband died."

"I'm sorry, señora. I picked a bad time to bother you."

"Come, here's the kitchen."

"I know, and this is the door to the bathroom. I lived here for eleven years."

The woman showed him the apartment and, in each room, Ricaño looked out of the window; all the windows faced the same street and at each one he paused a bit, as if the different views brought back different memories. When they entered the teen's room she immediately took her little sister to the next room. Finally, they went into the bathroom. The first thing Ricaño noticed were the floor tiles; he sat on the edge of the bathtub to get a better look at them and said to the woman, "I remember every single mark on these tiles! Look at this one. It looks like the head of a dragon, and this one's an old man with a cane...do you see it?"

The woman leaned over to look at the mark on the tile. He said to her, "Look at this one...what does it make you think of?"

"I don't know...a sailboat, maybe."

"Exactly! You can't imagine how many fights I had with my brother over this mark! He insisted that it was a shark, because of this stripe here, but it was clear to me from the beginning that it was a sailboat."

"It could also be a shark."

"What about the fin? I always told my brother that it needed a fin to be a shark."

"Here it is," she said, pointing to a slight excrescence on the tile.

"Too small!" He laughed. "You're worse than my brother."

Then the girl poked her head in but didn't have the nerve to enter.

"Hey you, come in here," Ricaño said. "Tell me what you see."

The girl came closer, looked at the mark he was pointing at. "I don't know," she said, and burst out laughing.

"Doesn't it look like some kind of animal?" her mother asked.

"Señora, you're trying to feather your own nest," Ricaño protested. The eldest daughter had also stopped in the doorway and was watching them.

"Rosario," her mother said, "look at this mark."

The teen, without looking at Ricaño, moved closer to look at the tile.

"What do you see?"

"It looks like a sailboat."

"You see?" Ricaño exclaimed.

"But it also looks like a shark," her mother said.

The teen studied the mark again and shook her head.

"No," she said. "It's missing a fin. It doesn't look like a shark."

"What did I tell you?" Ricaño burst out and caressed the cheek of the youngest daughter, who immediately grabbed for her mother's skirt and asked to be picked up.

Her mother did so and, with her daughter in her arms, she asked Ricaño, "Where do you live?"

"In Australia. In Melbourne."

"Where the Olympics were held?"

"Well, they were in Sydney, señora, but the Olympics were also in Melbourne. In 1956."

The woman nodded, then said, "Would you like a cup of coffee?"

Ricaño glanced sideways at the eldest daughter and took her distracted expression to mean he had permission to stay.

"I'd love one, but I've already taken up so much of your time."

"It will only take me a minute," the woman said.

They moved to the kitchen. Ricaño sat in a chair and the woman put coffee in an espresso pot, put it on the stove, and lit the burner. The teen scolded the girl for getting too close to the stove. Ricaño asked the woman how long they had been renting the apartment, and she told him two years.

He nodded and said, "We had a table that looked a lot like this one, señora, but in that corner, not here."

"I've told her that a million times," the teen exclaimed, "but she won't listen to me! She says there's not enough light in the corner."

"Truth be told, señora, you'd have a lot more space, and you'd be surprised about the light, there's more than enough."

"What's the point of making any changes now?" the woman asked.

"Mamá, the 'For Sale' sign has been up for six months!" the teen replied. "It could be another six before it sells." And turning to Ricaño she asked, "Will you help me, señor?"

"With what?"

"Move the table."

"If your mom doesn't mind..."

"Do what you want," her mother said and turned off the burner under the espresso pot. Her daughter went to the table, Ricaño stood up, the two of them cleared it off, removed the tablecloth, and carried it to the corner farthest from the window.

"Look, señora, how much space you have now," Ricaño said.

"Sure, but the table's in the dark," she replied.

"It's because of the fridge, but if we put the refrigerator here, like we had it, the table will have plenty of light."

He and the teen struggled to move the fridge while the lady of the house poured the coffee into two cups. Indeed, without the fridge in the way, the table had plenty of light.

"It looks a lot better," her daughter said.

"That's how it was. It was just like this!" Ricaño exclaimed, observing the kitchen's new layout.

He took the cup of coffee the woman offered him and sat back down. He was sweating after moving the fridge. The teen wanted to know which room had been his, and when Ricaño answered that it was the same one that she and her little sister slept in, she asked him if they had arranged the beds the same way.

"No, we had them at an angle. I can show you if you want."

They moved to the girls' room. Ricaño showed them how his bed and his brother's had created a square between one wall and the other.

"That's weird! You could sleep like that?" the daughter asked.

"If you think about it, it's the best way to place them. If you do, you'd have enough room for a desk."

"Where?"

"Here," Ricaño said, opening his arms to indicate the space. The teen envisioned the room's new layout immediately and looked at her mother.

"Ma, it can't hurt to try. Let's take advantage of the fact that this man can help us. If we don't like it we can put everything back the way it was."

"Do what you want. I'm going to get more coffee," her mother said and went back to the kitchen. Ricaño and the teen removed the books from the bookcase so they could move it more easily and then they moved the two beds. By the time they finished, the woman had come back from the kitchen and sat down on one of the beds. She hadn't brought any more coffee. Ricaño was breathing heavily; moving the bookcase and beds had been more difficult than moving the refrigerator. The teen was the most cheerful.

"There's even enough room for a small bookcase," she said. "We can put it here."

"Better over here," Ricaño suggested, pointing to the nook next to the window.

"Enough!" the mother exclaimed, irritated, and stood up. Her daughter turned pale and asked her what was wrong, at which her mother looked at her angrily. "What's the point of moving the furniture around if we're going to leave? And you, Señor Santibáñez—"

"Ricaño," he corrected.

"Ricaño, or whatever your name is...you come here and move everything around, because when you were a boy the table was there and the bookcase here, and the bed just so...You and your childhood!"

"Señora, I—"

"You only came here to make trouble!" And she turned and walked out of the room.

Ricaño looked at the teen, who sat on the other bed and seemed to have lost all her enthusiasm.

"My mother is touchy," she told him. "Three months ago today my father died."

"Yes, she told me."

"She's right. Why rearrange everything if we're leaving? You should go."

Ricaño stood up, approached the window, and looked out at the street, fogging the glass with his breath. He was still breathing heavily from the work he'd just done. He turned to the teen and said, "Ask your mother if she'd like me to put things back the way they were."

The teen went to the kitchen. He heard them arguing. When the daughter reappeared she said dryly, "Leave everything as it is."

He left the room, went to the apartment door, and tried to open it, but it was locked with the little chain. The daughter unlatched it, opened the door, and Ricaño walked out onto the landing. The door slammed shut behind him and he stood there motionless, back turned to the door he'd opened and closed countless times; he started to walk toward the five stairs that led to the entryway, went down them, walked to the doorway, opened the door, and went out to the street; he crossed to the café on the other side, went up to the bar, and ordered an espresso. From the bar he looked once again at the windows of his old apartment. He imagined the mother and daughter arguing, uncertain whether to leave the things as they were or to put them back like before. He had done them a favor and they had kicked him out. At least he would have liked to know if they were going to follow his suggestions. Maybe they wouldn't change anything now, but the next day, in the morning, seeing things with fresh eyes, they'd put everything back in its place and all his efforts would have been in vain.

He drank the espresso in two gulps, went to the phone, which was next to the bathroom, and dialed the real estate agent's number. The woman he'd spoken to an hour before answered.

"This is Santibáñez," he said.

"Yes, Señor Santibáñez, how may I help you?"

"I just saw the apartment," he said. "After speaking with you I remembered an appointment I have this afternoon, and since I was already here, I decided to take a look. I rang Señora Del Valle and she kindly showed me the apartment."

"And what did you think?"

Ricaño cleared his throat. "I liked it a lot," he said.

"I'm glad," the woman said.

"But you know, it's hard to have a whole picture of a place if you've seen it only once."

"I understand, you'd like to take a second look. How about tomorrow afternoon, four o'clock?"

"Yes."

"I'll see you tomorrow then, at the entrance to the building."

"See you tomorrow," Ricaño said, hung up, went to the bar, and ordered another espresso.

mothers and dogs

Around noon on Monday Luis called from Cuernavaca to tell me Mamá had had another episode and the doctors wanted someone from the family to spend the night with her in the hospital. We'd been taking care of our mother for three weeks, ever since she'd become ill, switching every forty-eight hours. Since it was my turn I told him I'd head to Cuernavaca right away, but Luis didn't think it made any sense for me to go all the way to the hospital since he was already there, and he said I'd be more useful if I went to his apartment and fed Ñoqui, his dog, who hadn't eaten for the last twenty-four hours. I told him I wasn't sure if the dog would remember me, because she'd only seen me once before. If she smelled you once she'll remember you forever, Luis said, and then he told me a few phrases I could say that would keep her under control: Sit! Go to your bed! Stay! And then he immediately explained where I could find the bag of kibble and how to clean the poop I'd most likely find in a corner of the bathroom or kitchen. I listened half-heartedly to his instructions, troubled by the thought of having to face his Neapolitan mastiff. Luis finished by telling me that Graciela, his ex-wife, had a spare set of keys to his apartment. He made me repeat the magic phrases back to him—Sit! Go to your bed! Stay!—and we hung up.

I called Graciela's office number and asked her when I could come by to pick up Luis's keys. She said she wouldn't be home until nine o'clock that night. I told her that nine o'clock was too late, because Ñoqui hadn't eaten for twenty-four hours. I can't before that, she said dryly, and I didn't insist, because I was thinking I'd ask her to come with me to Luis's house. The dog knew her well, or at least better than me. I knocked on her door at exactly nine o'clock. I hadn't seen her for a year. She had the

16

keys in her hand when she opened the door, and she handed them to me immediately, with the clear intention of not inviting me inside. We'd never gotten along. She had a new haircut that accentuated the severity of her gaze. If you'd come with me, you'd be doing me a huge favor, and I explained that Ñoqui had seen me only once. Ñoqui doesn't like me, she said. She doesn't like you, I said, but at least she knows you; she's only seen me for five minutes of her whole life. I hate that dog, she's out of her mind! she exclaimed. She hadn't asked how Mamá was doing, and I sensed her inner satisfaction that I was afraid of Ñoqui. I'll be fine without your help, I told her, turning away, certain that we'd never speak to each other again. I went down the stairs and heard her close the door.

Luis's best friend was Fernando; he probably knew the dog, so I looked for his number. No one answered and I left a message. The phone rang a while later. It was Luis. He told me Mamá was still stable. I asked him if that was good news and he said he didn't know. Did you feed the dog? he asked. I just went to Graciela's house to pick up the keys; I came to my place to eat a sandwich and now I'm going to feed her, I answered. He asked why I hadn't gone to feed her as soon as I left Graciela's place. I sensed that he was annoyed but the only thing that occurred to me to say was: I'm hungry, too, not just the dog! Luis, then, asked if I was scared and I immediately blurted out: Yes, Graciela says the dog is crazy, so I'm calling Fernando to see if he'll come with me!

Listen to me, he said, first of all, I'll remind you that Ñoqui hasn't eaten for thirty-six hours. Luckily, she can drink from the toilet. Second, Fernando's on a trip, and third, I know my dog. She's not crazy, Graciela's the one who's crazy. I wouldn't have asked you to feed Ñoqui if I thought she might attack you. She's smelled you once already, and when you call her name, she'll calm down right away. So she's upset? I asked. She's not upset, she's probably just a little nervous, Luis answered. We were quiet. Our squabbles had the dynamic of a cockfight: an explosion of feathers and screaming, followed by a kind of stupor. I asked him about Mamá again and he said she was sleeping. That's how I'd like Ñoqui to be, I said. It was a stupid thing to say, but it cracked Luis's facade a bit because he seemed to remember the duty of the firstborn to take care of their younger siblings. It's okay, he said, go to that park that's a few blocks from my apartment tomorrow morning around eight o'clock; you'll see a guy with a boxer; we're friends and Ñoqui knows him well because we see each other every morning when we walk our dogs; ask him to go with you. I don't know his name, but the boxer's name is Istanbul.

I dreamed about dogs all night: Ñoqui, Istanbul the boxer, my neighbor's fox terrier, later Graciela appeared and asked me if I was afraid Mamá would die and I told her yes, I was, but that I'd get by without her help. I woke up really early and got to the park by Luis's apartment before eight o'clock. I sat on a bench and waited. Half an hour later I saw the boxer. I got up, walked over to the guy, and asked if his dog's name was Istanbul. He said yes, and I told him I was the brother of Luis, Ñoqui's owner, and we shook hands. He asked about our mother. Stable, I replied. Then I explained the situation, emphasizing that Ñoqui hadn't eaten for forty-eight hours. If the dog has smelled you once, no problem, he said. She's never seen me, I lied. He told me that he had an appointment in half an hour and could only join me that evening. Not until tonight? You can't before that? I asked. Impossible, he answered. We agreed to see each other at ten o'clock in front of Luis's building and, as I said goodbye, I petted the boxer.

I silenced my cell phone so I wouldn't have to talk to Luis, who'd be furious if he found out I wasn't going to feed Ñoqui until ten o'clock that night. Every now and then I'd check it to see if I had a call from him. Since he didn't call me even once, I thought Mamá was still stable.

I had a horrible day; I couldn't stop thinking about Ñoqui, that she was hungry, drank water out of the toilet, and I looked at my phone every thirty minutes. I should have been more worried about my mother than the dog, but Mamá was in a hospital, surrounded by doctors, while Ñoqui was alone and hungry.

I arrived at Luis's apartment building at half past nine, exhausted from a day of absolute inaction. I waited on the sidewalk for Istanbul's owner and after twenty minutes I knew he wouldn't be coming and that he was also afraid of Luis's dog. It was one thing to see her every morning in the park, walking beside her owner, and another to have to face her alone. I thought I had no other choice but to face Ñoqui. My neck ached I was so nervous as I rode the elevator up, and when I put the key into the lock, Ñoqui ran up, slammed into the door and scratched at it furiously. At least she's still alive, I said to myself. She'd caught my scent and knew I wasn't Luis. I spoke to her through the door but that only made her growl more. It wasn't true that she'd calm down by calling out her name, like Luis had assured me. As I walked down the stairs, I turned on my phone to call and ask him to come to Mexico City, because the state his dog was in, wild with hunger, there was no way to get into his apartment. But Luis didn't answer and I went back to wondering if something had happened to Mamá. I called him one more time before I went to bed but his phone was turned off.

I didn't sleep a wink. I'd lost track of how many hours the dog had gone without food, so I got up at half past four in the morning and went to Luis's place, determined to face her. Maybe, I told myself, so early in the morning with the city still asleep, my encounter with her would be more affable.

I went up in the elevator and when I inserted the key in the lock I didn't hear any growls. I was afraid Ñoqui was dead. Then I heard footsteps inside the apartment and thought Graciela had felt sorry for me and was feeding the dog. The door opened, but it wasn't Graciela, it was Luis.

What are you doing here? I asked. He looked sleepy. I came to feed Ñoqui, he answered. I asked him when he'd arrived. An hour ago, was his reply. And you left Mamá alone? He turned around without answering me and told me to close the door. I closed it and followed him into the kitchen. Would you like some coffee? he asked. I said no. He started to wash a glass in the sink and said, Mamá died. Just then the dog appeared, I jumped back by instinct, she came to sniff me, wagged her tail, and left the kitchen; she stopped in the hallway and looked at me as if demanding an explanation for why I hadn't come to feed her. When? I asked without taking my eyes off Ñoqui. Seeing her so docile I felt ashamed of myself. Monday around noon, Luis said. But that was two days ago! I exclaimed. He sat down at the breakfast table, looked out the window, and said, Had I told you, you would have run to Cuernavaca, without feeding Ñoqui. I was going to tell you as soon as you'd fed her.

He stood up again, opened the fridge, and poured himself a glass of juice.

You wouldn't have brought Mamá back to life running to Cuernavaca, he continued. You were needed more here, feeding the dog. But you were scared.

I just wanted to come with someone! I exclaimed. Graciela didn't want to come with me and your friend with the boxer stood me up, but I'm here now. I was going to open the door, you saw it!

He sat back down at the breakfast table. I sat down, too. The silence was sudden. Mamá had died. What did the rest of it matter?

Did you cremate her? I asked.

I watched over her all night in the hospital chapel. The next day I made the arrangements for the cremation. I tried to delay things because

I wanted you to see her, but they have their rules and she had to be cremated when it was her turn. I haven't slept a wink in two days.

He put his arms on the table and laid his head on them, as if to go to sleep. I watched him and wondered if I wouldn't have acted the same way. I'd spent the previous day thinking about Ñoqui, that she hadn't eaten in three days, and only once or twice about Mamá.

Luis raised his head, stood up, went to his room, and came back with a porcelain container that he placed on the kitchen table.

Her ashes! he said and put his head back on his arms. It was starting to get light outside. I looked at the container for a few minutes, without opening it.

Make me some coffee, I said, and I lit a cigarette, but Luis had already fallen asleep.

lying in the sun

There was a knock at the backyard door. He got out of the lawn chair where he had been sunbathing and told himself that it couldn't be Rodolfo, the gardener, because it wasn't Tuesday, the day he came to cut the grass. Besides, Rodolfo wouldn't have knocked because he had the keys to the house. He opened the door and saw a woman with indigenous features, a Bible in her hand and wearing a wide-brimmed straw hat that contrasted with her thickset build. A Jehovah's Witness, he thought. He

25

was surprised by her mature age and that she was alone. Jehovah's Witnesses were almost all young and moved about in pairs.

"I'm not a believer," he blurted out politely to free himself from the intruder. The woman smiled as if she were accustomed to hearing these words.

"I come to bring you the news of our Lord Jesus Christ," she said, wiping her forehead with a handkerchief. Despite the heat, she wore woolen stockings, a skirt that covered her knees, and a blouse buttoned up to the base of her neck.

"I'm not a believer and I'm sunbathing," he said, as if it were some kind of curative treatment.

"It's wonderful that you can enjoy the sun! Praise the Lord for such joy," she said, still wiping her forehead, and he noticed the marks her sweating fingers made on the cover of the Bible. She was a robust woman, and she wasn't going to faint from the heat, but he felt obliged to ask if she wanted a glass of water. The woman smiled.

"Thank you, I could really use one," she said.

As he crossed the yard he thought that it would be more courteous of him if he offered her the glass of water on the porch and not in the street, under the sun, like a thirsty animal. He retraced his steps and, without going all the way to the gate, he told her to come in. The invitation, from that distance, acquired a rather compassionate character, with the door open so she could leave at once.

The woman walked through the doorway and followed him to the porch. He went to the kitchen and reappeared with the glass of water.

"Bless you!" she said and drank the contents in one gulp.

"Can I refill that for you?"

"If it isn't too much trouble," she replied averting her gaze, and he understood that it made her uncomfortable seeing him in a bathing suit.

He went to the kitchen to fill the glass with water, returned to give it to her, and pulled one of the porch chairs closer to her. "Rest for a moment."

The other thanked him and sat down. She looked exhausted. He noticed more acutely the contrast between his half-naked body and her attire, and he felt self-conscious.

"Take your time," he said, and he went back to the lawn chair, where he lay on his stomach. He had shown her that he was indifferent to her religious beliefs but not to her thirst or her weariness, and he was pleased with himself. He imagined that she was a widow, with married children she hardly saw, free to devote herself body and soul to that ministry in second-rate towns. His back burned and he realized he hadn't put on any sunscreen. He got up and went back to the porch. He had left it on the table. The woman was still sitting, the glass of water in her hand.

"How nice that you can enjoy a yard like this!" she said, drinking the last sip of water.

"Yes," he said, and he started to smear the sunscreen onto his arms.

He would drive ninety kilometers to lie in the sun for half an hour, then take a cold shower and go back to the city. He did it two, sometimes even three times a week. Raúl and Margarita were in France for six months and had left him the keys. He knew his way around the house perfectly because they often invited him over.

As he was smearing the sunscreen on his other arm, he was again assaulted by the embarrassment of being in his bathing suit in front of this woman in her woolen clothes, and he felt like he should put on his shirt. But then she asked him if he wanted her to rub the sunscreen on his back. He looked at her, not quite sure he had understood her, and stammered, "Yes, of course."

The other stood up, left her Bible on the chair, and he handed her the tube and turned around. He felt the awkwardness of her rough hands, which contrasted with the delicacy with which she spread the white substance across his back, and he was grateful that she had smeared the sunscreen on her hands first instead of squirting it directly onto his skin, like Luisa did, which always gave him an unpleasant shiver. Her extremely timid movements revealed that this was the first time that she had ever smeared sunscreen across someone's back, and he couldn't help smiling. She noticed and stopped suddenly.

"Am I tickling you?" she asked.

"No, not at all."

She smeared a new dose on him with the same exaggerated squeamishness, but now he could no longer control his laughter, and she blushed and pulled her hands away from his back, as if she had been caught in the act of committing a sin.

"Forgive me," she said mortified, and closed the little tube of sunscreen.

"Don't pay any attention to me. I'm laughing because I remembered a joke," he said, but the woman didn't seem to believe him and asked if she could wash her hands. He led her to the ground-floor bathroom and, returning to the porch, put on his shirt, which he had left on a chair.

The woman returned a few minutes later and pulled *The Watchtower*, the official magazine of the Jehovah's Witnesses, out of her bag and told him, "I hope you will take time to read this."

It was clear that she was in a hurry to leave. He took the magazine, walked with her to the gate, and they said goodbye.

Four days later he was back at Raúl's house. He lay down on the lawn chair in his swimsuit, expecting to hear someone knocking on the gate at any moment. He hadn't stopped thinking about the woman's calloused hands, which had rubbed that balm onto his back with such unprecedented slowness. Not even Luisa, in the best moments in their brief relationship, had ever touched him in such a way. He got up twice to open the door to spy into the street, and he extended his stay in the yard two hours. When he went inside to shower off, he left the bathroom window open so he could hear if someone knocked at the gate.

He returned a few days later, but he didn't realize it was Tuesday, so he ran into Rodolfo, the gardener, who was mowing the lawn. He wasn't going to lay in the sun with Rodolfo working in the yard, so he told him that he had only come to pick up a few books he needed. They talked for a while and he asked if he knew a woman who was a Jehovah's

Witness, a rather stout, middle-aged woman who wore a raffia hat. Rodolfo informed him that the Jehovah's Witnesses often came to the village, especially on Saturdays, to take advantage of the influx of people from the capital coming to their weekend homes, and that he didn't know any of them. He picked up a few random books, said goodbye, and got into his car.

He returned on Saturday. The sun was already beating down when he tossed himself onto the lawn chair, and fifteen minutes later he heard someone knocking. He went to open the door. It was the woman, with the same hat as the previous time, and a little girl was with her. She told him the girl was her granddaughter. The little girl didn't have a hat and he reproached the woman: "How can you bring her along without a hat in this sun?"

He told her that they should come in and he offered the girl a soft drink, though she only wanted a glass of water, and the woman accepted another. He went to the kitchen and returned with the two glasses of water. Suddenly he regretted inviting them in. If the woman had come alone, he would have thrown himself on the lawn chair like before, letting her drink her glass of water on the porch and after, why not, he would have asked her to rub sunscreen onto his back again; but now, with the little girl there, it was out of the question. He wondered if she had brought her granddaughter to protect herself because she had liked rubbing the sunscreen on him and she was afraid of her own desire. As if he had read her thoughts, the woman told the girl to hurry up and drink her water because they had to leave.

"Let her rest for a bit," he said, and he entered the house, went to Julito's room, opened the closet, and rummaged through the bottom drawer until he found the boy's red cap. He thought no one would notice it was missing because Julito never used it. He knew that house better than its owners. Margarita always asked him if he remembered where they had placed one thing or another, from the mosquito repellent to her husband's shorts, and he always got her out of a pinch. He was the expert at killing the scorpions that appeared frequently throughout the house. He wasn't afraid of them, and while Raúl and his family positioned themselves at a safe distance, he crushed them with the first thing he could get his hands on. Sometimes he wondered if that wasn't why he was invited so often and, of course, for Julito, who had made him his eternal playmate, with the obvious approval of his parents, who were thus able to attend to their visitors. He went back to the porch with the cap and put it on the girl's head.

"Do you like it?" he asked her.

The girl nodded.

"You can keep it."

"Tell the gentleman thank you," the woman said to her granddaughter.

The girl murmured a thank-you and, attracted by a crow hopping across the grass, she wriggled her hand out of her grandmother's and left the porch to follow the bird. They both stared at her.

"I wanted my granddaughter to see this yard, that's why I brought her," she said.

He turned to look at her and said, "This isn't my house; it belongs to some friends who are traveling."

"I know, it's Señor Raúl's house."

"You know Señor Raúl?"

"Who doesn't know him? With all the fuss he's caused in this town!"

"What fuss?"

"Don't you think it's a fuss that he thrashed the mayor?"

He was bewildered for a few seconds. Raúl hadn't told him anything. He thought his friend came to shut himself up in his house without developing even the slightest relationship with the people in the town, like most of the people did who had their weekend homes there.

"I've only seen him once, and from a distance," she added. "A colleague knocked on his door once

33

and Señor Raúl slammed it in her face. He's got quite a temper!" And she laughed, as if she thought it was funny. "I knocked at the gate because I knew the señor was traveling and that he had hired someone to look after his house for him."

"I'm not looking after it; he loaned it to me," he said, feeling a sudden dislike for the woman.

She had pulled a magazine out of her bag. It was the same edition of *The Watchtower* as the last time. "Here," she said.

"You already gave me one," he exclaimed dryly, "don't you remember?"

"Oh, good," she said, without asking him if he had read it. Suddenly he understood: The portly woman could neither read nor write. She went from door to door, despite her age, because she occupied one of the lowest rungs of the organization, if not the lowest. She was an ordinary soldier in the ranks, with infinite faith in the word of the Lord. And yet she hadn't made the slightest attempt to preach to him. She had told him how lucky he was to be sunbathing in that yard and she had rubbed sunscreen on his back. He wondered if she had done it because she knew he wasn't the owner of the house but someone who was looking after it, and the blood rushed to his face at the thought of her feeling sorry for him.

"Thank you for the water," she told him, and she called her granddaughter. The girl ran back to the porch and he accompanied them to the gate.

He watched them walk down the gravel road and closed the gate, and he knew that the woman wouldn't be coming back, because she had managed to enter the house and show it to the girl.

He stared at the tabachín tree, the pine, the small grove of ficus trees, and the rosebush in the back, and he wondered if coming there every three or four days to lie in the sun was not some response to the zeal with which he had assumed the role of caretaker Raúl had subtly imposed upon him. For the first time he suspected why Luisa had left him. It had to do with this house, where she had seen him move around, perfectly aware of what was in every closet, every drawer, in every cupboard, always ready to repair any little damage and play with Julito. Suddenly she had stopped coming around and one day she called to tell him with the utmost delicacy that everything was over between them. With the same delicacy with which the woman had rubbed sunscreen onto his back.

on the track

Rudy Alatorre runs three afternoons a week on the athletic track two blocks from his house. He considers himself lucky to have a sports center so close by. Alternating running, jogging, and walking, he completes eight laps around the all-weather track that surrounds the soccer field. At sixty-four, it seems like the right thing to do. His orthopedist has told him that his lumbar vertebrae can't take prolonged exertion and advised him to follow a medium-intensity routine, which Rudy Alatorre follows to the letter.

He arrives at the sports center late in the afternoon, when the dusk light gives way to the track lights, which are turned on gradually and reach full power in less than a minute. He likes the contrast between the nocturnal atmosphere created by the floodlights and the last of the day's light left in the sky, and often, while running, he plays with the idea that instead of dusk, it's dawn. The first and second lanes are for the exclusive use of the fastest runners, or those who consider themselves as such. As the lanes expand outward, they are occupied by those who run more slowly. Rudy Alatorre uses the fourth, the one exactly in the middle. When a fast runner comes upon a slower one in the same lane, he shouts *"Pista!"* so the other will get out of the way and move out of the lane, but it's not always the case that the slower runner reacts properly and there have been confrontations that, fortunately, haven't escalated into something serious, at least not the ones Rudy has seen.

Our man doesn't talk to anyone, although he recognizes many runners who frequent the oval track at the same time he does. Only those who belong to a team or one of the sport center's associations, recognizable because they wear the same uniform, joke with each other; most only know each other by sight, start running after warming up for a few minutes, and, when they finish, gather their things and leave.

Rudy has jogged two laps at a moderate pace and now he moves to the fifth lane for his walking lap. Once that one's finished, he returns to the fourth lane and begins his steady-trot laps, which represent the most intense part of his workout. His body is fully warmed up and at this point his breathing is a heavy panting. It's the most painful part but also the most exciting. He's a little out of it while he runs, all kinds of images tripping over each other in his hyper-oxygenated brain, leading his mind down strange paths.

He's surprised that the lights around the track haven't turned on. The track is immersed in a nocturnal twilight and the lines on the track are the only reference he has to stay inside the lanes. Night has fallen without him noticing. Someone approaches, running in the second lane, and shouts out *"Pista!"* which always causes some uneasiness among the runners, and even more so now that you can hardly see anything. Rudy Alatorre thinks that the delay in turning on the lights might be a result of the change to winter time. Whatever it is, it gives him a strange thrill to run with the floodlights off, his panting mixing with the gasps of the other runners, whom he can hardly see. It seems to him that his athletic cadence, efficient but monotonous, has given way to a more urgent rhythm, as if the darkness has made something atavistic emerge in those running on the track. He notices it in the giggles of the men and women who spring up around him, and they make him feel like he's not running alone but in a herd. The glow coming from the office situated at the north curve dimly illuminates that part of the track and the rest is submerged in darkness. Rudy thinks that if he were to trip and fall, the others would step on him. Still, he doesn't slow his trot, afraid of losing contact with the herd.

He hears a scuffle behind him, followed by the thud of someone's fall. Someone exclaims "Well done!" and then a woman's laughter. In the adjoining lane another woman shouts "That'll teach 'em!" and Rudy Alatorre realizes he has lost count of the laps he has run; for the first time since he's started coming to the sports center, he feels like he has stopped running in circles and has a goal, although he doesn't know what that goal is. He hears another ruckus behind him and someone pushes him, trying to get by. Any other time he wouldn't hesitate to get out of the way, but in the darkness enveloping the track it can be dangerous to move sideways, so he stays in his lane. He's pushed again and he feels someone scratch his neck. He realizes that she is a young woman, stiffens his body so she can't pass, and when she shouts "You old fuck!" he elbows her and hears her cry of pain followed by the empty thud of her fall. "Well done!" someone running beside him exclaims, and there's more laughter. Rudy knows that a horde has formed in the darkness; their footsteps and uniform breathing give him an intoxicating sensation he hasn't experienced since he was a child. They had just left the north curve behind them when they hear an impetuous stride approaching from behind. They know that sound well, the sound of overflowing youth. "Give it to him good!" someone exclaims, and the horde invades the first lane. The runner screams when they run into him, then he falls and rolls on the all-weather track. "Well done!" the gentleman next to Rudy exclaims triumphantly. "We've had enough!" one of the women says, a sixty-something he recognizes in the dark by the way she jogs.

The moon has just emerged above the trees and Rudy Alatorre has the sensation that he's not running on an all-weather track but crossing a forest during a night raid on enemy terrain. He's never run so oblivious to his lumbar vertebrae, and when he hears the impact and fall of another runner, he exclaims in a low, joyful voice, "That'll teach 'em, fuckheads!"

Seconds later his feet collide with something; he ends up facedown on the ground, but while he was falling he took the sixty-year-old woman who was in front of him down, too. He thinks they tripped over one of the fallen runners. Someone beside him whispers "You old fuck," and Rudy Alatorre recognizes the voice of the young woman who scratched his neck at the same time he gets a kick in the stomach that makes him double over. "Old fuckers!" a male voice exclaims. The blows raged down on them and the sixty-year-old woman let out a whimper of pain. Two guys lift Rudy up and hold him. "Don't let him go!" the young woman orders, now holding a stick in her hand. In that moment the floodlights on the north end of the track are turned on. "They turned on the lights!" one of the men holding Rudy exclaims. The young woman turns to the floodlights that begin to illuminate the track, exclaims "You're in luck, you old cunt!" and, throwing the stick down, she runs away, followed by the two young men, who leave, though not before throwing Rudy to the ground. He lies on the all-weather track, breathing heavily, while the others start to get up. His lumbar vertebrae hurt like never before. One of the women, the oldest, has a bloody shirt, doesn't look at anyone, and starts to trot away, limping a little. A tall man, after reaching the soccer field, has thrown himself down on the grass. His face is covered with blood, but no one approaches to see what's wrong. One after another, taking advantage of the semi-darkness in which the oval track is still submerged, they trot away, each in their respective lanes. Rudy Alatorre also goes back to his, the fourth one, the one right in the middle. He has been running with unusual intensity and, in addition to his vertebrae, his stomach hurts. He lost count of the number of laps he has run, but his body, enriched by two years of exercise, tells him that the hardest part is over and all that's left is loosening up, jogging the slowest lap, which he calls the orthopedist's lap.

nitric cellulose

My father had sold everything: dental instruments, car parts, life insurance policies, beach-apartment time-shares, orthopedic braces, and products that prevent baldness. He had no need to write business letters until he entered the nitric cellulose business, the orders of which could not be made by telephone, primarily because the pharmaceutical laboratories that are used in the elaboration of surgical binding agents were extremely punctilious in their requirements; therefore, it became necessary for Mamá to take over the business correspondence. She did this at home and Papá delivered the cellulose orders in his truck.

The high quality of the raw material and the reliability of his deliveries earned my father a good reputation, but I'm sure that his business wouldn't have prospered without Mamá's elegant and cordial letters. I was attracted to certain recurrent formulas, which I eventually learned and recited to myself, like this one: "Confident that our product will satisfy your refined requirements, we are at your service for new and fruitful accords." I'd go to bed with these words in my ears, "fruitful accords," thinking that it was worth living in a world where there are fruitful accords. And even when no fruitful accord was reached, Mamá's letters transmitted a fervor that renewed my faith in human co-existence, like in this closing phrase: "Lamenting the present impossibility of arriving at a mutually satisfactory solution, please accept herewith the assurance of our unaltered esteem."

Only those letters signed by Engineer Ramírez, director of Advanced Fabrics, Inc., could compete with Mamá's. Without losing one iota of commercial efficiency, they were impregnated with a shroud of gloom, with phrases such as: "Unfortunately, the shipment is held up at customs for sanitary verification procedures, where, with any luck, it will remain for only two weeks. Such is the bureaucratic red tape that interrupts our time!" They were the only letters Mamá respected and, as soon as she recognized the Advanced Fabrics letterhead in the daily bundle of correspondence, she separated their envelope from the others to open it.

"Who writes them, the engineer or his secretary," she wondered after reading those letters.

"I'm sure his secretary does, and she also signs them to speed things up," I replied.

Engineer Ramírez's signature was a very simple stroke that could be imitated easily.

"She must be a thin, petite woman," Mamá concluded.

"No, she's fat and has a double chin," I replied.

After a blood clot burst in her brain, Mamá slept a lot; the doctor told us she needed to rest, and Papá and I tried not to make any noise so we wouldn't wake her. I told Papá that he should buy me a manual so I could learn to write business letters. I wanted to take over the correspondence, while Mamá recuperated, but he didn't want me to, because I was supposed to focus on school. He wouldn't even let me help him take down the order information when he spoke with clients on the phone. I felt both angry at and sorry for him, watching him take those calls. He'd mix up the quantities, and more than once, when he delivered the order, they returned the product, pointing out that the formula was incorrect. And while the business foundered, Mamá slept and we weren't supposed to make any noise.

I would flee from that capsizing ship in the afternoons and go to Susana Bermúdez's house; she was three years older than me and had been my best friend when we lived in the same building, before we moved. When she told me that she might start working in the evening as a secretary in a law firm, I felt faint. I cried and she hugged me. We were on the living-room sofa, her mother had gone to the supermarket, and at some point she put a hand on my breast and squeezed it gently, then she slipped it into my cleavage and held it there, meanwhile she stroked my hair with her other hand. It didn't bother me, or I lacked the strength to refuse her and, somehow, I knew that this was going to happen. Susana never talked about boys.

Back home, I found the electric Olivetti on the dining-room table, where Mamá, before her blood clot, typed her letters. I asked her why she'd taken it out.

"I was practicing this morning."

She sat down again, turned on the machine, and awkwardly threaded a sheet of paper onto the roller. She started to type, searching for each key with her index finger. It took her a full minute to compose the phrase "We are hereby pleased to inform you..."

"There you go, little by little," I told her, trying my best not to burst into tears.

That night Papá came to my room and told me that the month before he had abandoned the cellulose business, because without Mamá's letters, with just the telephone, it was impossible to fill the orders; now he was selling Ping-Pong tables and he didn't need to maintain any kind of correspondence for that.

"Have you told her?"

"No. If she finds out I abandoned cellulose because I couldn't rely on her help anymore, she'll get worse."

"You're right, don't tell her."

"But she's going to find out once she sees there are no more order letters coming in."

"I can write fake letters and she can answer those," I said. "If she keeps practicing that might help her get better."

"She's going to find out."

"We'll see."

This time he didn't tell me that I had to focus on school.

I started my forgery work in Susana's house. I took letters from our old clients and between the two of us we cut the letterhead off the original letters and pasted it on a blank sheet of paper; then we made a dozen photocopies of each sheet. They looked authentic; I threaded the first one onto the roller of Susana's electric typewriter and started to type. It didn't take much effort to mimic the style of Papá's clients, which was really bland. To make my imitation more convincing, I made several spelling mistakes. The only ones I didn't dare to imitate were the ones from Advanced Fabrics. Mamá would have noticed right away. I typed six letters and Susana imitated the signatures. She was really good at copying a signature. She would look at it for a while, and suddenly, as if she were possessed, she would draw an identical one.

"How do you do that?" I asked her as I collated them one by one. She got up and, standing behind me, wrapped her arms around me and plunged a hand into my cleavage and then squeezed my breast.

"Do you want to see mine?" she whispered in my ear.

I told her *no* very gently, because I was afraid she wouldn't invite me back to her house.

"Silly girl," she said, kissing me on the back of my neck.

I took the six letters home so Papá could see them. He looked them over and said, "I don't like this game."

"It's not a game. We're doing it so she feels useful again."

"What if she realizes they're fakes?"

But Mamá didn't notice. That same afternoon she began to type her responses. It took her an hour to finish the first one. She showed it to me and I turned my back to her so she couldn't see my face while I read it. There was nothing left of her old style. But her spelling was still flawless.

"Is it that bad?" she asked.

"No, it's all clear," I said.

"What is it then? The important thing is that it's clear, right?"

"Of course," I said without turning around to look at her.

I found one of her old letters and read it in my room, in secret. Once again, I was captivated by her way of moving between data and the chemical specifications like an acrobat maneuvering around obstacles, injecting subtle humor into each line. That was missing now: the elegance and humor that, I was certain, were the principal elements responsible for the success of so many transactions.

It took her two days to respond to the six letters. When she finished, I had a new supply of fake letters ready and I went to Susana's house to have her sign them. When she opened the door she looked depressed and I asked her what was wrong.

"I didn't pass the law firm's exam," and she started to cry in my arms. I stroked her hair without saying anything. "Are you happy?" she asked, lifting her face from my shoulder, and she kissed me, sticking her tongue between my lips. But I kept them closed. She could do whatever she wanted with my breasts, but she needed to leave my mouth alone. She kept at it, and when she realized I wouldn't give in she moved away abruptly.

"If you're going to act like a little girl, don't even come over," she snapped. "Take your letters and get out of here."

I grabbed the letters and walked out. She had twisted my wrist so I would open my lips and only afterward did I feel the pain. While I was waiting for the elevator she opened the door and said to me in a voice choked with tears, "My house is your house, Mónica. I love you," and then she slammed the door shut.

That night, when Mamá went to bed after practicing on the Olivetti, my father told me, "She looks happier."

It made me angry that he didn't realize how fundamentally changed Mamá was since her blood clot. I didn't answer him.

I wrote down the phone number for Advanced Fabrics and the next day, during a break at school, I called the office. A woman's voice answered and I asked to speak with Engineer Ramírez.

"Father or son?" the woman asked.

"The one who writes the business correspondence," I replied.

"I write the letters," she said. "I'm Engineer Ramírez's secretary. With whom do I have the pleasure?"

I told her that I was the daughter of Señor Meneses, the owner of Celnitric, Inc., and I asked if we could meet that afternoon. She asked me what it concerned.

"It's about my mother. She's the one in charge of Celnitric's correspondence."

I told her it was a personal matter and that I'd rather see her outside the office. She was quiet for a few seconds, then she gave me the name of a coffee shop that was half a block from Advanced Fabrics and said we should meet at six.

"That's when I leave work," she clarified.

I arrived a little before six and sat at a table by the window so I could see the street. A woman crossed from the opposite sidewalk, saw me through the window, and waved. I waved back. Mamá was right, she was short. When she sat down across from me, I estimated that she was more than seventy years old. She introduced herself as Carmelita Suárez.

"My mother is very fond of your letters," I told her.

"And I hers, they are the best I have read in more than forty years in this line of work."

She had a firm voice, which contrasted with her fragile appearance. I told her about the blood clot in Mamá's brain and her slow recovery. She was visibly moved. I brought one of Mamá's recent letters with me and took it out to show her.

"This is how she writes now," I told her. "You be the judge." She read the letter and gave it back to me.

"It looks like a different person wrote it," she said.

"She *is* a different person!"

"What can I do for you?"

"Write her," and I told her about the spurious letters that I wrote in Susana's house. I could imitate the style of all of them but hers, which were Mamá's favorites and the only ones that could bring her out of her lethargy.

"You overestimate me," Carmelita said. We were quiet. She looked onto the street, took a sip of her tea, and said, "If a few of my letters can help your mother recover, you can count on me, but I will not send them through the mail, because forging a signature is a crime. You will have to come and pick them up yourself."

I told her that was precisely what I had in mind, because I didn't want my father to find out that I had gone to see her, and she asked me why.

"Because he thinks we're deceiving my mother."

She smiled for the first time. "I'm afraid your mother has already realized the letters are imitations. I would notice immediately, whomever they're from, and your mother seems to have a very fine eye."

I didn't know what to say, and she continued, "I have breakfast here every day. Tomorrow you can collect my letter from Consuelo." She pointed to a woman standing behind the cash register. "You can also leave your mother's letters with her."

She wrote her home telephone number on a piece of paper, for anything else I needed. I saw that her hand was trembling. She looked me in the eye and said, "I'm sick."

I felt stupid for not asking what was wrong, but I didn't dare. She gave me the piece of paper and we hugged as we said goodbye.

The following afternoon I went back to the coffee shop for her letter, which Consuelo removed from the drawer under the cash register. I read it on the bus ride home. It was, without a doubt, a letter from Advanced Fabrics. There was no shortage, amid the technical specifications on cellulose, of the ubiquitous apologetic flair: "We vow to complete our delivery punctually, though today this adverb, unfortunately, has lost its validity among raw material suppliers."

When I got home Mamá was typing in the dining room. I grabbed the bundle of correspondence, into which I secreted Carmelita's letter, and pretended to look through it in front of her. I exclaimed suddenly, "Look! A letter from Advanced Fabrics arrived."

She looked up and stopped typing, opened the envelope, read the letter twice, folded it slowly, and asked me, "Who wrote this letter?"

"What do you mean who?" I blushed. "It's a letter from Advanced Fabrics! Don't you see the letterhead?"

"You didn't write this letter!" she exclaimed.

"Of course not! Why would I write it? Why are you asking me that?"

She looked at me without answering, and I understood. Carmelita was right. Mamá knew that I was writing them.

"How did you know?" I asked.

"I've known all along."

"That's what Carmelita said, that you'd surely noticed."

"Who's Carmelita?"

"Carmelita Suárez, the secretary at Advanced Fabrics." And I told her that I'd gone to see her to ask her to write a few letters in her unique style, because I didn't feel capable of imitating them.

She covered her face with her hand and began to cry. I went over to her and we hugged.

"If you knew that I'd written them, why'd you write responses?" I asked her.

"So that you and your father could see me doing something." She recovered immediately and asked me, "What's she like?"

"Thin and petite."

"I told you so. I won."

"Yes. She told me that in all the years she's been doing this your letters are the best she's ever read."

She moved away from me, went to the table, and turned off the Olivetti.

"Don't turn it off. You should send her a reply. She made the time to write you, she deserves a response," I said.

"You write her back. You know how to write these letters now."

"Me? I just copied a few sentences and changed the syntax here and there."

"And how do you think they're written," she said.

I replied to Carmelita's letter, imitating Mamá's new style, or rather her lack of style, which was all I could imitate, and when I left school, I went to give the letter to Consuelo, who told me that Carmelita hadn't eaten breakfast there for two days. I didn't know if I should leave the letter or not. Consuelo decided for me, taking it out of my hand and putting it in the drawer under the cash register.

That night I called Carmelita's house but no one answered. I called again the next day with the same result. Mamá hadn't turned the Olivetti back on, but she hadn't taken it off the dining-room table either, as if she didn't want to part with it.

On Friday I went back to the coffee shop to see if Consuelo had any news for me. She told me that Carmelita hadn't been there all week, then she took my letter out of the drawer and said, "I'd better give it back to you."

I left the coffee shop and didn't know what to do. I decided to cross the street and walked in the direction of Advanced Fabrics. The doorman asked to see my ID and directed me to the third floor. I rode the elevator up with the letter in my hand. The Advanced Fabrics door was at the end of a narrow corridor at the center of the building. I rang the bell and an old man with a cane opened the door. I assumed it was Engineer Ramírez.

"Good afternoon. I'm looking for Carmelita Suárez," I said. He looked at the letter in my hand.

"What do you need?"

"I'd like to deliver this letter to her on behalf of Celnitric, Inc."

"You can give it to me."

I gave it to him, and he read the name of the sender.

"Since I had to come this way, my father asked me to give it directly to Carmelita, to save time," I told him.

"Come in, there's a draft."

I went in and he closed the door, directed me to a chair in the small lobby, which was separated from the rest of the establishment by a glass wall, and told me to sit down. He sat in another chair, took the letter out of the envelope, and began to read it. When he finished he said, "Carmelita died last night. She was very sick. She worked with me forty-three years. I always prayed to God to take me before her, but that prayer was ignored."

I said nothing, frightened by the sound of my own heartbeat, and I was afraid the old man would hear it in the silence that permeated the lobby. The thought crossed my mind that the letter Consuelo had given me was the last one Carmelita had written in her life.

"I'm no longer in charge of the business. The one who runs it now is my son," the old Ramírez said. "I only sign the letters, and that's why I remember the name Celnitric. It's a nice name."

"Thank you."

He looked at the letter and said, "I will give it to my son when he returns from the funeral."

"No, don't give it to him, it's a fake letter."

He frowned. "Why fake?"

I explained that it was a simple exercise, because Carmelita was teaching me how to write business letters. I had brought it for her to read.

"So you wrote it."

"Yes."

"How old are you?"

"Sixteen."

"And what are you studying?"

"I'm in my last year of high school."

He nodded and said, "The secretary who will step in for Carmelita is her niece. Her spelling is horrendous, and her syntax is atrocious. Your spelling and syntax are good. It's obvious that you had an excellent teacher." I thought that he was talking about Mamá, then I understood that he was referring to

Carmelita. He stood up, leaning on his cane. "Come to work in the afternoons. Two hours is enough, and it won't take much time away from your homework. You will be responsible for the correspondence; Carmelita's niece will take care of the rest."

"I should talk it over with my parents," I said, and again feared he would notice my heart palpitations.

"If it's okay with you, I will speak with your father, so we can reach an agreement about your salary. You are too young to negotiate your fees."

I went home, but I don't know if I was more stunned by Carmelita's death or by the job that Engineer Ramírez had just offered me. I'd drafted the letter imitating Mamá's new style, the only one I could imitate. What kind of style was I going to use for Advanced Fabric's correspondence, if I started to work there? Until now I'd only written business letters imitating the style of others. I didn't know what mine was, if I even had one.

When I opened the door, Papá and Mamá were sitting in the dining room. I could tell from their expression that they were waiting for me. I guessed Engineer Ramírez had spoken with Papá and I was afraid he had rejected the engineer's offer, arguing that I needed to concentrate on my studies. At that moment I noticed that the Olivetti was no longer on the table.

"The typewriter?" I asked.

They looked at each other and Mamá said to me, "We put it in your room."

"Why?"

"You're going to need it."

I smiled, excited, and Mamá stood up to hug me. Later, in the kitchen, she told me the monthly salary Papá had negotiated with Engineer Ramírez. It was very generous for only two hours a day.

That night, when they turned on the TV, I locked myself in my room, wound a sheet of paper onto the Olivetti roller, and caressed the keys. My fingers were trembling. I wanted to use my new work tool, to write something, anything, but I didn't know what.

I sat like that for a while, and suddenly, in one go, I wrote my first letter:

To the refined attention of Susana Bermúdez,

We would like to inform you of our current inability to fulfill your delicate requests. Various reasons oblige us to do so. Regretting our inability to reach a mutually satisfactory solution, please accept the assurance of our unwavering esteem.

Sincerely,

Mónica Meneses

on the other side of the fence

Jorge cursed and swore that his ball had landed on the line and not outside it, as Fernando maintained, but the latter dug in his heels. It wasn't the first time they'd argued heatedly about a point. Jorge lost his temper, pulled out the ball he had in the pocket of his shorts, and whacked it over the country club fence. Fernando's eyes followed the trajectory of its arc, and when he saw it land in the courtyard of a house on the other side of the street, he shook his head, furious. Now they'd have to stop the match to get it back because they'd only brought three balls.

After leaning his racket against the net Jorge left the tennis court, walked in front of the locker rooms, across the club's lobby, and went out to the street wearing his shorts, tennis shoes, and T-shirt. He was still angry and, instead of walking to the corner to cross at the traffic light, he crossed right there, even though it was a dangerous part of the street. He had to wait a minute before he found an opening in the traffic so he could cross to the opposite sidewalk. Once there he walked about a hundred meters until he reached the two-story house and rang the doorbell. The little gate with green grating was open, a sign that there were people in the house. When no one answered he rang again. He toyed with the idea of leaving the ball where it was and that way getting back at Fernando, who had purchased the three balls the day before. He was about to ring a third time when a woman's voice asked who was there. He turned his head but didn't see anyone. The small courtyard was full of plants, he looked up at the second-floor windows, but he didn't see anyone there either.

"I came to pick up a tennis ball that was hit over here from the club, señora," he said energetically, not knowing to whom he was speaking.

"In this house we no longer return tennis balls," the voice replied.

Then he saw the woman to his left, in a corner of the courtyard, beside a ficus. She was leaning on a cane and Jorge estimated that she was in her sixties.

"I can see the ball from here, señora," he said, pointing to a flower bed in the courtyard. "If you let me in, I can grab it in no time and then I'll leave."

It wasn't true that he had seen it; he said it so the owner of the house would give him permission to push the little gate open and enter her modest courtyard, where he was sure to find the ball right away. The woman advanced to the flower bed with irritating slowness and stopped.

"I don't see any ball," she said.

"My mistake. I thought that stone was the ball. But if you give me permission to enter, I'll find it in less than a minute, I promise."

"In this house we no longer return tennis balls, but you have the face of a decent young man, so come in."

Jorge pushed the gate, which squeaked open. The woman turned around, telling him to follow her, and started walking toward the house. When Jorge didn't move, she stopped.

"Didn't you hear me?"

"Señora, I'm sure the ball is around here some-where," Jorge said pointing to the flower beds next to the fence.

"Look for it later, now follow me," and since he still didn't move, she stopped and turned to look at him. "Are you afraid of an old woman?"

Jorge hesitated for a moment, then he followed her to the back of the house. She opened a door and they walked across a large, sunny kitchen, went into the living room, and the woman pointed to a sofa. "Sit down."

"They're waiting for me in the club, señora."

"Sit down for a minute, nothing's going to hap-pen to you."

Reluctantly, Jorge sat down on the sofa.

"Would you like some tea?"

"No, thank you."

The woman called out in an imposing voice, "Margarita!"

A young woman wearing an apron appeared. She couldn't have been more than fifteen years old.

"Make some tea," the woman told her. "There's hot water on the stove."

"Señora, I only came to get—"

"Do you take it with or without milk?" the owner of the house interrupted him.

"What did you say?"

"Whether you drink your tea with or without milk."

"Without, but look—"

"Did you hear that, Margarita? Without milk. Bring me a glass of water, and quickly, because the young man is in a hurry," and seeing that he had stood up, she told him to sit down again, and then she turned to the maid, who stood there motionless. "What are you doing standing there? Did you turn to stone?"

The young woman put a hand over her mouth to stifle her laughter and, turning around, she went back to the kitchen.

"Don't pay any attention to her, it looks like that blockhead likes you," the woman said, sitting down on a little armchair in front of Jorge, and she asked him his name.

"Jorge."

"Like my son," she said, and she stared at him as if sharing the same name as her son prompted her to look for a resemblance between the two of them. She must not have found one because she looked away and said, "Jorgito returned the tennis balls that landed in our courtyard. He had a strong arm. He always managed to throw them over the club fence. He loved to do that."

He merely nodded his head. He thought that Fernando would be wondering why he was taking so long to come back, and he loathed that crippled woman who was keeping him in her house.

"Jorgito, because of his problem," she continued, pointing at her head, "never had any friends or went to school. His whole life in this house, taking care of me! He'd only go out that door to pick up the tennis balls that dropped in from the club, and he'd throw them back immediately. He had, like I told you, a strong arm."

The young maid entered at that moment holding a tray with the tea, which she placed on the coffee table while looking at Jorge out of the corner of her eye; she raised a hand to her mouth to stifle her laughter and ran back into the kitchen.

"Don't pay attention to that silly girl, help yourself, there's the sugar," his host told him.

Jorge spooned a little sugar into his cup, stirred it, and looked in the direction of the courtyard, hoping that his gesture would remind the woman why he was there. The other asked him how old he was.

"Seventeen."

"Jorgito's the same age."

He began to suspect that she was crazy and that there was no Jorgito. He imagined that Fernando would be cursing him for taking so long, because there was another pair of players waiting their turn on their court, and that delay gave them the right to occupy it.

"Should I tell you how it all happened?" the woman asked him and, without waiting for his response, she detailed what occurred: "A ball dropped. I don't know how he did it, but wherever he was, Jorgito knew that a ball had just dropped into the courtyard. He went out to pick it up, and the moment he was going to throw it back he noticed the palm tree in the street. Before they turned it into the awful central roadway it is now, this was one of the most beautiful and quiet streets in the neighborhood. There were palm trees down the middle, like many of the streets in this district, but you're too young to remember that."

It wasn't hard for him to imagine the central flower beds dividing the traffic lanes lined with palm trees. Maybe he had seen them as a child. He had always lived in that neighborhood.

"And what happened?" he asked, pretending he was interested so the other would finish her story.

"He realized the palm tree was too high. He'd already told me: The palm trees are too high, Mamá. And that day he had a feeling he wouldn't be able to throw the ball over it. He did something he'd never done before: He opened the front gate and went out to the sidewalk. He was forbidden to do so, but he disobeyed me, taking advantage of the fact that I was upstairs. He thought it would be easier to throw the ball from the street."

He imagined Jorgito calculating the correct angle for his throw and guessed what came next.

"Of all the decisions he could make, he made the worst one," she said, "crossing the street to throw it from the opposite sidewalk. I heard it all from my room: the screeching tires and then the thump. I stopped cold."

He looked at her. Maybe she was younger than he had estimated, but the grief and isolation had aged her prematurely. He took another sip of tea and set the cup back on the saucer.

"Señora!" the maid called from the hallway.

"Excuse me, I'll be right back," the woman stood up and left the living room, leaning on her cane.

Jorge looked at the furniture. The furnishings seemed to be from another era. There was a record player like the one his family had had in their house for many years; his father had later given it to the handyman who waterproofed their roof. Five minutes later, seeing that the woman wasn't coming back, he stood up and called out timidly, "Señora?"

The house was immersed in a camphorated silence, one from another time. The street traffic was barely audible.

"Señora?" he repeated, leaning into the hallway. He heard the servant's giggling coming from the upper floor and the voice of the owner of the house, who scolded her about something. Without hesitating, he went into the kitchen, crossed it, and went out into the courtyard, walked to the gate, and started searching for the ball among the plants. Almost immediately he heard a voice behind him.

"Is this the one you're looking for?"

He straightened up with a start. The fat teenager in the wheelchair was showing him the tennis ball. His gaze seemed slightly dislocated, and his mouth was lower on one side.

"I thought you were dead!" he said to him.

"What?"

"Aren't you Jorgito?"

"Jorge," the teen corrected.

"Nice to meet you." He held out his hand, but the other ignored his gesture and told him, "In this house we no longer return tennis balls."

"I know, but I spoke with your mother and she said that this one, in particular, you are going to return."

"Why?"

"Because your mother and my mother are close friends, you didn't know that?"

"Who's your mother?"

"Señora. Santibáñez."

"I don't know who she is. Who are you?"

"Jorge, we're namesakes." He extended his hand once more and the other left him with his hand in the air again, so he completed his gesture by snatching the ball out of the other's hand. The teen, despite his portliness, had quick reflexes, grabbed him by the arm and Jorge felt his strength. He certainly did have a powerful arm. They started to wrestle, and he had to let go of the ball. The fat kid spat in his face, which made him set his scruples aside and push him, wheelchair and all, into the flower bed. The chair tipped over, the kid rolled out and fell flat onto the concrete where he lay motionless. He didn't cry out at all. He picked up the ball, pushed open the front gate, and left the house. Once he was on the sidewalk, he was unable to take another step. If the other had shouted or screamed, he would have run away, but his silence held him beside the fence. He heard one of the chair's wheels swishing as it continued to spin, looked back at the little gate, which he had closed; he opened it again and went back into the courtyard. The fat kid still lay on the ground motionless, as if meditating on the best way to get up by himself. Jorge stopped the spinning wheel and righted the chair, then he bent over him and put his hands under his armpits. The other avoided looking at him, locking his eyes on the courtyard tiles. "Loosen up and hold on to my neck," he ordered him, and the teen obeyed. For a moment he was afraid the other was going to strangle him. He lifted him suddenly, holding him against his body, and managed to deposit him in the wheelchair. The effort left him gasping for breath. The other one was also breathing heavily.

"Take me inside," he requested, and Jorge didn't know if he should listen to him or go through the little gate and take off. He saw that the other had a scratch on his cheek that was bleeding. He remembered that the kid had spit on him and he wiped his arm across his face to clean it off.

"Take me inside," the fat kid said again.

He stood behind him and pushed the wheelchair. They entered the kitchen and when they crossed the hallway that separated the kitchen from the living room, the teen's mother was coming down the stairs. She was holding on to the handrail, followed by the young maid, who was carrying the cane.

"I was upstairs with Margarita," the woman said. She didn't seem surprised to see them together. "What did you do to your face? The ficus again?" she said when she saw the scratch on her son's face.

Jorgito nodded, laughing.

"You're such a klutz," his mother said. "And what about you, kiddo? You have a scratch on your neck, too. What happened to you?"

"He didn't see the ficus!" Jorgito exclaimed, roaring with laughter.

"One's clumsier than the other," the woman said in a cheerful tone.

They went into the living room and she exclaimed, "But young man, you haven't finished your tea…Margarita!"

"Yes, señora?"

"Heat up this tea, it must be ice-cold by now."

Jorge didn't have the strength to contradict her. The maid took the tray back to the kitchen and he sat down on the sofa. Deep exhaustion numbed his limbs and he thought it was caused by wrestling with Jorgito and the strain of getting him into the wheelchair.

The owner of the house asked him, "Do you want to take a nap in my room? Go upstairs and sleep a little, I'll wake you in half an hour."

"Fernando is waiting for me…they want to play on our court…"

His eyes were closing. Jorgito looked at him, laughing. He caught a glimpse of his mother motioning for him to keep quiet. The young maid, who had just entered, held the tray with the tea and she was also laughing.

Someone shook his shoulder and he opened his eyes. Fernando was leaning over him with a finger pressed to his lips, ordering him not to make any noise, and he asked him in a low voice why he was asleep in that house.

"I got sleepy," Jorge answered. "How'd you get in here?"

"I rang the bell but nobody answered," Fernando said, "but the front gate was open, and so was the door."

"Did they see you?"

"Who?"

"The señora and Jorgito."

"I didn't see anyone. Stand up and let's get out of here."

Only then did he seem to realize that it wasn't a dream and that it was a real Fernando speaking to him. He tried to sit up, but he was too shaky. "I feel dizzy," he said.

"Hold on to me."

He held on to the arm of his friend, who helped him stand up; they walked slowly to the door and went out into the courtyard. He looked up because he felt like he was being watched from one of the second-floor windows, but he didn't see anyone.

"Those cowards are upstairs!"

"Cowards? Why?"

"They put something in my tea to put me to sleep. Go ask them for the ball."

"Forget the ball. Let's get out of here."

Fernando opened the gate and they left the property. He felt like shouting "Cowards!" in the direction of the upstairs windows, but he was dizzy, and he let himself be carried away by his friend, who held on to one of his arms so he wouldn't fall, a gesture he found touching. Fernando had a bad temper, but he was a loyal friend. He asked him if he'd had to cede the court to the two guys waiting their turn to play.

"Yeah. Since you were taking so long, I told them that they could use it, and I came to see what had happened."

"We can play them in doubles," he said, stopping abruptly.

"Look at you. You're in no shape to play. What'd you do to your neck?"

He felt the scratch near his throat and remembered his scuffle with Jorgito.

"I scratched myself on a ficus in the courtyard."

"Why'd you take so long?"

"The señora offered me tea."

"Tea?"

"I couldn't say no, she has a retarded son in a wheelchair. That maid put something in my tea because I suddenly felt groggy."

"You felt groggy because you were out all night partying. I need to get some sleep, too."

They stared at each other and Fernando suddenly looked at him as if seeing him for the first time.

"Why are you looking at me like that?" he asked.

"It was my fault," his friend said.

"What was your fault?"

"That you had to come and look for the ball and that we lost the court. I tricked you."

"You tricked me?"

"Yeah, your ball wasn't out. It hit the line."

the dutch

Every morning the two Dutch families took a small inflatable boat out for a short ride around the lake. They went as far as Los Conejos, a little tree-lined island that could be seen from the trailer-park beach. The boat had a fifteen-horsepower Evinrude outboard motor. My father, who had been toying with the idea of buying an inflatable fishing boat for a while, said it was a reliable motor, less flashy than the Mercury but nobler, more durable, and still, after so many years, those two names, Mercury and Evinrude, represent, in my mind, two opposite ways of being.

Each Dutch couple had a twenty-year-old daughter and, if I remember correctly, the two families were spending their vacation together at the lake because their daughters were close friends. Even though they were twice my age, I was in love with one of them, the more ordinary one, clearly an Evinrude person. The other, blond and extroverted, was an all-out Mercury creature and a real head-turner, but Evinrude, if you paid a little more attention, showed herself to possess a discrete and impeccable beauty that, in the end, overshadowed the somewhat conventional charms of her friend.

My father and uncle would come to the lake on Saturday, and early Monday morning they'd go back to Milan. During the week, with the two men away, the Dutch families took us under their protective wing, communicating in English with my mother and aunt, who spoke it with some difficulty.

My aunt, that morning, had taken my brother and cousin to town and I stayed behind with my mother, who tried in vain to convince me to go with them. Why don't you go? she repeated angrily, and I didn't understand why she was so insistent. Those trips to town bored me and I preferred to stay in our tent reading a book. Soon after, about to depart on their morning boat voyage, the Dutch asked us if we wanted to go with them to Los Conejos. My mother said that any kind of watercraft made her sick, but that I would love to go and, taking the book from my hands, pushed me toward the shore so I could get into the boat. I think it was Mercury who took me by the chin and said a word in Dutch that made the others laugh. It was something about my eyes. Mercury and Evinrude were always admiring my eyes. The fifteen-horse motor started, discharging a cloud of smoke, and my mother waved to us from the shore. We hadn't gone more than two hundred meters when one of the men made clear to me that I could stand beside him to control the rudder. I sat at the stern and held the Evinrude rudder handle firmly, but I had difficulty keeping it steady, the boat veered to the left and by the time I straightened it out I had drawn a full semicircle with it. Now the boat was heading back to the shore we had just left a minute before and everything seemed to indicate that I had made that maneuver so I could return to my mother. I didn't dare look at the Dutch, who merely smiled, friendly like always. Instead of trying to make them understand that the abrupt swerve was the result of my clumsiness with the rudder, I remained impassive, adjusting my expression to the appearance of the facts. We reached the shore and the Dutchman stopped the boat so I could get off. I said, "Thank you very much" in English, and the six waved their hands goodbye. Embarrassed, I walked to our tent and when I entered I was surprised that my mother wasn't there. I thought she'd gone to buy something in the trailer-park supermarket, so I picked up my book and went inside the tent to read, not having the courage to look at the Dutch as they moved away in their boat.

I fell asleep, lulled by the rhythm of the train. It was night and I was traveling to Amsterdam. At the Copenhagen glass fair I'd bought two glass-blowing machines from a Dutch manufacturer, and the company's deputy director, a lanky man who insisted on speaking to me in Spanish, had invited me to visit his factory in Amsterdam, hoping that I'd want to expand my order. I told him it wouldn't be possible because I had a tight schedule and that same afternoon I was going to Paris. In Paris everything went faster than I'd anticipated; I had three free days before I had to return to Mexico and thought about changing my plane ticket to move up my trip, but I remembered the Dutchman's invitation. I thought about it for a few minutes and went to my hotel, paid my bill, and took the train to Amsterdam that night.

I stayed at the hotel the lanky guy had recommended and the next day phoned him to arrange a meeting. He bought me lunch and then took me to his factory, where I purchased the latest macerator model and several replacement pieces for the injection band. I didn't really need the macerator or the replacement parts; I only bought them to give the whole thing the appearance of a business trip, because my real purpose was to look for the two Dutch families. My mother and one of the two women, I think it was Evinrude's mother, had sent postcards to each other for one or two summers; my mother saved her correspondence in a shoebox; maybe she had saved one of those cards and it had the woman's address on it. It was a crazy idea to look for the Dutch after so many years, just to tell them that the only reason I didn't go to Los Conejos Island with them that morning had been my clumsiness with the rudder. When I'd tell them that I'd taken a train to Amsterdam to clear that up, I'd look like a madman.

Back at the hotel I called my mother, and I was afraid she wouldn't remember the two families. Three years before she'd had a stroke, a portion of her memory had evaporated and maybe the Dutch were in that part. When she answered the telephone, I told her that I happened to be in Amsterdam on a business trip and that it had occurred to me to look up the Dutch from Lake Garda. I asked if she remembered them.

"Why wouldn't I remember them?" she replied, offended.

I asked her to look for the address of one of the two families in her old letters.

"But how are they going to remember you if you were a nine-year-old boy?"

"Ten years old," I corrected her, and added, "If we remember them, why wouldn't they remember us?"

My mother despised thinking about the past and I suspected that her stroke had been a worthwhile way for her to throw out most of her memories. However, she continued to hold on to all of her correspondence, a mountain of letters that she may have used only to remind herself that she had a past.

"Let me see if I can find something. Give me half an hour," she said dryly.

When I called her back, she had good news: She'd found three postcards from Karla, that was the name of one of the two Dutch women, and on one of them she'd written her Amsterdam mailing address. She dictated, letter by letter, the woman's last name and the name of the street, and then she said, "I'm sure they're already dead. They were old people."

"Maybe I'll find the daughters." And I reminded her that each family had a daughter in her twenties, both of them really beautiful.

"I know. Your father couldn't take his eyes off of one of them."

I asked her which one, and she exclaimed, "How am I going to remember that? Why are you asking me all these questions?"

I couldn't bring myself to tell her I was curious to know which way my father leaned, toward the Evinrude or the Mercury.

We hung up, I went down to the reception desk and showed the manager the name of the street. He circled the location on the map and recommended that I walk there even though it was a bit far. That's what I did, and after twenty minutes I entered a pedestrian area full of shops, much brighter than the other streets. Night had settled there before the rest of the city and for a moment I thought about giving up my search for the Dutch and staying on that cobblestone sidewalk that glowed with the intense tones of a movie set. I stopped in the middle of the flowing crowd and noticed that the people could barely contain their excitement, as if they'd come to do something less than honorable. Some of them, however, began to stare at me, as if stopping violated some unspoken rule, so I walked on and wound up leaving those cobblestones where I glimpsed who knows what kind of potential for a turbid demise.

The street where the Dutch lived was short and the building I was looking for was close to the corner. The entryway was unassuming; I read the names beside the apartment buzzers and, when I saw Karla's, I panicked. What was I going to tell them? Assuming they remembered me, how could I tell them about that morning when, because of the Evinrude's rudder, I hadn't been able to go with them to Los Conejos Island? It would be better to turn around, go back to the cobblestone street, and mingle with the crowd. I'd tell my mother that the Dutch no longer lived at that address. I moved a few meters away from the door to take a last look at the building, turned around, and started to walk, but I stopped, knowing that I'd never forgive myself for having come so far and leaving like this without at least trying. I could see myself remembering that evening in Amsterdam and being disgusted with myself for my lack of courage, so I went back to the door and rang the doorbell.

A few minutes passed before a burly man with the face of a Turk opened the door and looked at me suspiciously. I showed him the card where I had written down Karla's name and address, he read the name and made a gesture with his fingers, which meant the third floor. I climbed the stairs slowly because I didn't want to be out of breath when I arrived at the door. I saw myself extending my hand to an old bent deaf woman. As I was climbing to the second floor I felt like I was being watched; I looked up and saw a middle-aged woman with black hair and extremely pale skin leaning over the railing. The Turk must have called and alerted her that I was coming up and she had gone out to see who it was. I climbed the last steps and when I was in front of her I couldn't decide if she was beautiful or not: Her eyes were big, black like her hair and sweater. I nodded my head slightly, showed her the card that I had presented to the Turk, and told her in English that I had come to look for that person, to give her greetings on behalf of my mother. She asked me, also in English, what my mother's name was; I told her and explained that the woman on the card and my mother had met in Italy, on Lake Garda, and I pronounced the name of the town where the trailer park was located. She lowered her eyes, rummaging through her memory, and that gesture brought her back to me completely. It was her, the beautiful Evinrude, and I stared at her, stunned. I was in Amsterdam, in front of the first love of my life. She raised her eyes and, as she handed the card back to me, said that Karla was her mother and that she and her father had died nine years ago, one a few months after the other. I nodded, looking regretful. She asked me if it was my first time in Amsterdam and I said yes. She looked at me with the hesitation of someone who can't quite reconstruct an image in her memory and invited me to come in.

The apartment was crammed with furniture and she led me to a sitting room, directed me to an armchair, and sat down in front of me, adjusting her skirt with a modest gesture that seemed to be from another time, like the furniture. I asked her name. Mariana, she answered, but she didn't ask my name and I thought that she was in a hurry for me to leave. She said yes, she remembered us, two young women with three boys, two women whose husbands, she added, came to the lake on the weekend, isn't that right? Yes, I said, encouraged by her good memory. She added that she particularly remembered one of the two men, a dark-haired athletic guy. That was my father, I told her, and she looked at me closely, as if trying to reconstruct the features of my father through mine, and I wondered if there hadn't been something between the two of them. Perhaps I was about to discover the remote cause, the first rustling of decay, that had ended in my parents' divorce when we moved to Mexico.

To break the silence that had gathered I uttered the word Evinrude, and explained, "Your boat had a fifteen-horsepower Evinrude outboard motor."

"What a memory you have," she said with some annoyance, as if suspecting she were in the presence of a lunatic.

"I have a memory tied to that motor," I said, and in my poor English I told her about the events of that distant morning, attempting to give an amusing spin to my story. I managed to, because she laughed for the first time and her laughter made my heart race.

"It's a memory that has haunted me until now," I told her, encouraged by her laughter, and when she stopped laughing, I saw her as beautiful as I had always remembered, with her Evinrude beauty, discrete and gentle, to the extent that I hadn't recognized her at first. "I think I came to Amsterdam just to tell you this story," I added, blushing.

She told me to wait a moment, got up and left the room. She returned with a cardboard box, which she placed on the coffee table. I saw that it contained several envelopes filled with photographs. She put on her glasses and started to rummage through the box. While she did so, I looked at her legs, which had that thickness that promises heavenly thighs, and I blushed again. She'd removed a bundle of photos held together with an elastic band and flipped through them one at a time, until she found the one she was looking for.

"Here it is!" she said, and she handed it to me, asking if I was the boy in it. I recognized myself, surrounded by the Dutch on the rocky shore of Los Conejos Island. I answered yes, surprised I didn't remember that excursion with them. I only remembered the trip that was aborted because of my clumsiness with the boat's rudder. I looked at the picture again. There was a dark man beside me, thirty-some years old, with black hair, whose face I vaguely remembered, and I asked Mariana who he was. "My cousin Philippe," she answered. That was the only time he had gone with them to the island, she said, because he got dizzy on the boat. One of Philippe's hands rested on my shoulder. He was quite handsome, a mixture of Evinrude demure and Mercury splendor. I could have sworn that he wasn't in the boat the morning I'd had the problem with the rudder, so that photo was from another excursion, before or after the ill-fated one.

"Of all of us, he was the only one who spoke French, that's why he communicated with your mother better than the rest of us," Mariana said, and she was quiet after that, looking at a photo she'd taken out of the stack. For a few seconds the photo became transparent with the lamplight behind her and I was able to make out a man and woman, their heads close together in a romantic gesture, he with dark hair and her light skin. When she saw that I was looking at what she had been looking at, she blushed and slid the picture behind the others. I realized that my intrusion had upset her. She reached for the photo with Philippe; I gave it to her and she put it with the others and then put the bundle in the envelope and put it back in the box, making it quite clear that the photo-viewing session had ended. She looked at me harshly and I saw a glimmer of the bitter woman she was, one who had lived her whole life with her parents, caring for them with resentment and devotion.

"I should go," I said, thinking that a few minutes before, if she had asked me to, I would have stayed in that house forever. I stood up; she got up to show me the way out, and when we reached the door I stopped to ask her about the man in the photo she'd hidden beneath the others, but Mariana, as if she had guessed my intention, extended her hand and snapped, "Thank you for your visit!" and I knew she wouldn't answer me. We shook hands coldly, she opened the door and closed it behind me. When I got downstairs the burly Turk opened the entry door for me, and as soon as I walked through he immediately closed it behind me with a heavy thud.

The streetlights had come on; I started to walk and Mariana's words about Philippe came back to me: "Of all of us, he was the only one who spoke French, that's why he communicated with your mother better than the rest of us." She had said "with your mother," without mentioning my aunt. It was surprising she remembered that only my mother spoke French. I was assaulted once again by that image of my mother pushing me along the lakeshore so I would get on the boat with the Dutch. When I got out of the boat after my abrupt turn of the rudder, she wasn't there, and she didn't reappear for another hour. Had I come to Amsterdam following a memory of that sudden disappearance? Was it her and Philippe in the picture Mariana had hidden? Suddenly I found myself on the cobblestone boulevard crowded with people, standing in the glow of the lights from the shopwindows. I stopped in front of one without noticing the merchandise on display. I walked on a few more steps, stopped again, and thought about going back to Mariana's house to ask her to show me the picture; I'd tell her that many things in my life depended on it and that my trip to Amsterdam would only make sense if I could see it. But I knew that I'd lack the courage to confront the Turk. I saw myself struggling with him and then violently thrown to the street. Maybe the one in the picture was him, pressing his head to Mariana's. Since I'd stopped in the middle of the sidewalk, people were walking around me angrily, and I started walking again, letting myself be carried forward by the crowd. The boulevard curved and it didn't seem as captivating as it had an hour ago, but noisy and crude. I remembered being told that many streets in Amsterdam form a semicircle, and I thought that because of another semicircle, the one I'd drawn with the Dutch families' boat, I was now right where I was.

at the regional bus stop

From the taxi that stopped on the highway at the regional bus stop, a man emerged wearing a corduroy jacket. When the taxi pulled away he saw a man with a Gladstone, a doctor's bag, across the road waiting for the bus traveling from the valley to the mountains. The heat was intense. The man in the corduroy jacket carried a little black umbrella, which he opened to protect himself from the sun. The other put his bag on the ground, sat on it turning his back to the sun, and covered his head with a handkerchief. They looked at each other briefly. They were alone, separated by the asphalt road, waiting for buses going in opposite directions.

The one in the corduroy jacket, sheltered by his umbrella, lit a cigarette. Minutes later, at the far end of the straightaway, the bus heading to the mountains appeared, the one the man with the Gladstone was waiting for, but he couldn't see it because he was sitting with his back to the valley. The bus was approaching the stop, and despite the noise of the engine, the one with the Gladstone didn't seem to notice it. The guy in the corduroy jacket cried, "Hey, your bus!"

But the other didn't flinch.

"Hey!" the one with the corduroy jacket repeated more loudly. The bus drove by and the man with the Gladstone, seeing it pass right beside him, got up and ran to catch it, only to watch it disappear around the curve. He remained motionless for a few seconds, then he turned his head toward the man with the corduroy jacket, who shook his head in a clear gesture of reproach. Responding to this gesture, the man with the Gladstone raised a finger to his ear and after that to his mouth and, crossing both fingers, closed them, to indicate that he was unable to hear or speak. Then he sat on his bag, this time facing the plain, and covered his head with the handkerchief again. Twenty minutes later another bus heading to the mountains appeared at the far end of the straightaway. It was coming closer, but the deaf man gave no sign of moving. The one in the corduroy jacket saw the handkerchief on the ground and realized that the man had fallen asleep. He shouted to get his attention, but then remembered that he was deaf. He looked for an appropriate-size rock, picked it up, and threw it, but missed. The bus slowed down a few meters from the stop and, not receiving any signal from the man with the Gladstone to stop, it accelerated again and was lost from sight behind the curve. The one with the corduroy jacket looked for a bigger rock, found one, and this time hit the other man's leg. The deaf man leapt to his feet; he looked at the one in the corduroy jacket, who had stooped over to grab another rock, and he also stooped down, using his bag for cover. At that point the bus coming down from the mountain appeared. The man in the corduroy jacket raised his arm to stop it a few moments before a stone the deaf man threw shattered one of the bus windows. The driver, who was slowing down to stop, immediately accelerated and drove on. The two men watched it zoom away toward the valley and looked at each other. The one in the corduroy jacket made a gesture of complaint at the one with the Gladstone, explaining

to him through his gestures how he had thrown the
stone to rouse him from his slumber (he pressed
both of his hands together under his cheek, inclined
his head, and closed his eyes). The man with the bag
responded by opening his arms, a gesture that was
both an apology and at the same time a reproach
for the blow he received from the stone and, lifting
his pant leg, showed the other one the wound on his
shin. The one in the corduroy jacket, annoyed that
he'd lost his bus, kicked a stone, which made him
cry out in pain; he limped a few steps away and sat
on the ground rubbing his foot. The one with the
Gladstone sat down on his bag again and looked
at his wound. The drivers of the few passing cars
could see two men sitting at the regional bus stop,
separated by a strip of asphalt, rubbing their lower
appendages.

The sky had clouded over, and the first drops fell.
When the downpour hit, the man in the corduroy
jacket motioned for the man with the Gladstone
to take refuge under his umbrella. The one with
the Gladstone crossed the road and the two hud-
dled together under that shelter, contemplating the
downpour without moving. In a way it was easier to
be like this than one in front of the other, glancing

sideways at each other. Suddenly, the deaf man
made a gesture to the man in the corduroy jacket
to tell him that he needed to attend to a certain
necessity and, covering himself with his bag, he
walked away, down the dirt path toward a ditch
filled with bushes. The man in the corduroy jacket
considered the problems one could have defecating
in that downpour, using a Gladstone as your only
cover, and he went after him, caught up with him,
and swapped the umbrella for the bag, something
the other thanked him for with another gesture.
The one in the corduroy jacket returned to the bus
stop with the Gladstone over his head, looked toward the valley and saw that the deaf man's bus was
coming. He yelled at the deaf man to hurry up, but
he remembered he was deaf. When the bus arrived
at the stop, he raised his arm, the bus stopped and
opened its door. He asked the driver to wait a little and ran to the ditch, where the deaf man was
shitting under his umbrella; he lifted the umbrella,
and, seeing that the other hadn't finished, signaled
the bus driver that he should wait a little more,
but the bus driver couldn't delay any longer and
shut the door; the bus drove away and the one in the
corduroy jacket saw it go around the curve, hardly
a minute before his bus, which was rushing down
the mountain, appeared, but he was too far away to

catch it. He cursed the deaf man and threw the bag on the ground. The Gladstone opened on impact. He crouched down to close it and saw two open eyes looking at him. He recoiled several steps in disbelief. He went closer and saw the human head. Several black clumps of dried blood had formed along the edges of the severed neck. He felt the urge to run away, but he stopped himself because the deaf man was standing up behind the bushes. He closed the bag. It had stopped raining. The other returned the umbrella and held out his hand so he would give him the Gladstone. He gave it to him, trying to conceal his panic, then they started to walk toward the road, the deaf man in front and he followed a few steps behind, without taking his eyes off the black bag.

Night had fallen and the few cars driving on the asphalt road had their lights on. Once again, they stood across from each other, each one waiting for his bus, but this time the deaf man didn't sit on his bag. At the end of the straightaway the lights of his bus flashed. When it was close, he raised his arm to stop it and said goodbye, with the same gesture, to the man in the corduroy jacket, who responded by nodding his head. The bus sped away, taking with it the deaf man, and the man in the corduroy jacket sighed in relief. Then he saw a shape on the ground.

He looked at it, cursed the deaf man, crossed the asphalt road, grabbed the Gladstone, and looked along both sides of the highway. He thought he could take it to the ditch and hide it, but he ran the risk of losing his bus, which was going to arrive at any moment. He rejected the idea of leaving it where it was. The bus driver he'd spoken to during the downpour had seen him holding the bag over his head and it was likely that he'd remember not only the Gladstone but also his face. He heard the sound of a motor and his bus appeared around the curve. He decided to take the bag with him, quickly crossed the highway and signaled for the bus to stop.

The bus stopped, its door opened, and he got on. The bus driver asked him, "Are you a doctor?"

"I beg your pardon?"

"I asked if you're a doctor," the man repeated, pointing at the bag.

The one in the corduroy jacket hesitated for a moment and answered yes.

"There's a woman in the back who feels sick. Go see her, and I'll take your fare later," he said and drove off.

the quarry

I shouldn't sweat, he said to himself. He remembered reading in "To Build a Fire" by Jack London
that sweat is your worst enemy on a really cold day,
because a damp body exposed to low temperatures
freezes more easily than when it's dry. Dawn had
broken with a lot of fog and all day the passing cars
had been driving around with their headlights on.
He'd been pedaling for more than half an hour in
the direction of the quarry, his eyes fixed on the
curb running along the avenue, and his regular

pedaling and the fog had plunged him into a pleasant hypnosis.

Suddenly the traffic diminished, a sign that he
had reached the first vacant lots of the suburbs. He
thought that it would have been prudent to turn back,
but he felt strong enough to pedal several kilometers
more and didn't want to break out of the tedium the
cold and low visibility produced in him. Farther on
he found the turn he'd been looking for. He followed
the dirt road and a few minutes later heard laughter
in the distance. Apparently he wasn't the only one
who'd had the idea of visiting the frozen pond. When
he reached the end of that stretch of road, he saw several bicycles on the ground. A little farther on, a few
boys were sliding across the ice that had formed on
the small lake in the quarry. Their shouts of satisfaction floated above them and they pushed one another
down on that slippery flat surface. He left his bike on
the embankment so it wouldn't be confused with the
others, and walked down to the ice, which he stepped
onto carefully, to test its strength.

He slid across it timidly and during the first minutes the other boys paid no attention to him. Then,
in one of his slides, he deliberately tripped and fell
butt-first onto the hard surface. The ruse worked,
because from that moment on they took note of him,
though not enough to ask his name.

When they got tired of that game they decided to go to the little island in the center of the pond, and they gathered sticks and branches to test the thickness of the ice. He took his place in the line and they advanced in single file over the thin layer of snow that covered the icy surface. Where the snow had melted and he could see the bluish water beneath the ice, the sight of the bubbles that the cold had immobilized in the midst of their rise from the bottom of the pond gave him an idea of its depth, and for the first time he was afraid. The initial revelry had made way for the patter of sticks with which all of them were sounding out the ice beneath their feet. He tried to step in the tracks of the boys in front of him and that way be certain that he was stepping on a firm surface, a trick he had learned from reading *Endurance*, which was about Captain Shackleton's journey to the South Pole. His feet were the only thing that stood out in the whiteness formed by the frozen ground and the fog, and he fell back into a pleasant numbness. How far he was from home! he thought, and stopped in the middle of the silence that he suddenly noticed surrounded him; he turned to look behind him and to the sides, he looked down in search of the footprints of those who were in front of him and saw nothing. I'm here! he shouted, as if responding to a call from the boys, but no one called out to him and no one answered him. He looked for his own tracks so he could go back, followed the trail for a few meters, and suddenly heard a cracking sound under his feet and stopped, stood there motionless. He'd read in Curwood's *The Alaskan* that the worst thing you can do when ice breaks is start to run; instead, you should walk with your legs a little apart to distribute your body weight over as wide a surface as possible. But he didn't know which way to go. He thought that any direction would be good, because it was a small pond, and he advanced for a hundred meters, testing the ice with the stick. The dog appeared out of nowhere. Black and huge, it looked at him as if it had been waiting for him. It wasn't wearing a collar, but he knew that it must have belonged to one of the nearby farmhouses. He stopped in his tracks and thought he could hear his own heart, certain that the dog could hear it, too. The animal growled, staring at him, and he averted his eyes, because he had read in Jon Krakauer's *Into the Wild* that when you have a sudden encounter with a wolf you should avoid looking into its eyes. The dog didn't move and it seemed to him that it felt uncertain of its footing on the icy surface. He thought that it was also lost, and when it barked, it sounded more like a call for help than a threat. He held out his hand, signaling it to stop in order to halt an eventual attack by the animal, and the dog watched him, as if intimidated by that fragile and solemn gesture. It panted with its tongue hanging out, then miraculously it turned its muzzle to the side and walked away, disappearing into the fog.

He tried to calm down, waited a few minutes, and resumed his march in the same direction as the animal, following its tracks and trusting that they would lead him to solid ground. A little later he spotted the outline of the embankment and made his way there carefully, because it was the least stable part of the ice surface. In fact, the icy layer had broken where it met the shore, forming a gap that was impossible to jump across. He plunged his foot into the water, felt the bite of cold and the miry bottom, then he sank his other foot in and with a little push reached the firm ground of the shore. He sat down on a rock to take off his shoes and socks, because he had learned in *Igloos at Night* by Hans Ruesch that if you fall into a frozen pond you have to take off your clothes to avoid hypothermia and gangrene. He rubbed his bare feet to circulate the blood and twisted his socks until the last drop of water was wrung out; he put them back on, put on his tennis shoes, and stood up.

He walked about a hundred meters along the shore looking for his bike, and then he retraced his steps and walked another hundred meters in the opposite direction. He saw the long snowless furrow he and the other boys had made as they slid across the ice and told himself that his bike should be close by. He surveyed the shore once again in both directions and finally accepted the fact that the boys had taken it.

He climbed the embankment to get a wider view of the area, but the fog was still really dense and he was only able to see bushes, rocks, and crisscrossed tree trunks. A few meters ahead, leaning against one of those trunks, he saw his bike. He remembered that he had left it there before he went down to the frozen shore. He picked it up, making sure that nothing was missing. It was intact. He pushed it through the rocks and bushes, careful not to make any noise that would attract the attention of the dog, which must have been nearby, and every so often he kicked his feet on the ground to get rid of the wet sensation creeping into his socks. Suddenly he spotted the asphalt road. He walked toward it, and when he got on his bike, he didn't know which direction to go. He pedaled slowly, dreading another encounter with the animal. The fog began to lift or he had become accustomed to looking through it, because he saw the bonfire when he was still twenty or thirty meters away. The man was sitting in a curious way, half squatting and half leaning over a paint can, holding his hands close to the fire and rubbing them together vigorously. He thought he might be the dog's owner. When he rang the bike bell, the other turned his head. I got lost, he said, and the man looked at him with the same bewilderment the dog had a few minutes before. He uttered the name of his street and asked him if he could show him the way back. The man told him that he'd been in the capital for only two months and wasn't familiar with the area; however, he was expecting his sister any moment, and she could certainly tell him how to get back. The man's behavior and voice calmed him; he got off his bike and pushed it toward the fire, and he sat down next to it to warm up. The other turned his attention back to the flames, as if he were accustomed to visits from the people who passed by on the roadway, and asked him where he was coming from. He told him from the quarry, where he'd walked over the ice to reach the island in the center of the pond with some boys, until he'd lost sight of them and had run into a big black dog, whose tracks led him back to shore. The man listened to him without opening his mouth, noticed that his shoes were wet, and told him to take them off to warm his feet by the fire. Obedient, he took off his sneakers and socks, put them next to the fire to dry, and rubbed his feet again. Only then did he notice there was a structure behind them, a kind of bunker with a large green door. He thought it was a factory and that the man must work there, maybe as a watchman. There was a sentry box, a kind of concrete capsule that protruded from the front wall, with a thin fissure that didn't deserve to be called a window. The man, at a some point, stood up, walked toward that bulge, and opened a door that he hadn't seen because it was the same color as the concrete, and he entered the gray structure, closing the door behind him.

He waited a few minutes for him. Seeing that he wasn't coming back he put on his socks, put his sneakers back on, and got up. He was attracted to the door, but by the way the man had disappeared behind it, as if the capsule had swallowed him, he preferred not to approach it. He picked up his bike and pushed it toward the road. He was about to get on it when he saw a headlight coming toward him. He heard the squeaking sound of a bicycle's brakes, and the voice of a woman uttered something vulgar. She was a voluminous, old woman wearing a heavy overcoat and she hurled him an angry look and asked what he was doing there. He replied that he was lost and didn't know how to get home. The other uttered another vulgarity, asked him where he lived, and, hearing his response, turned and looked up and down the road, as if orienting herself. You should be locked up inside your house in this cold, why did your parents let you go out, she asked. He was about to answer that they were always fighting and that's why he had taken his bike and headed to the quarry, but he didn't say anything, hoping that the woman would feel sorry for him and help him get out of there. The other said, Follow me! and she told him to keep his eyes on the red taillight on her rear-wheel mudguard. She started pedaling slowly, and he pedaled after her. The woman's silhouette intimidated him, and he wasn't sure if he should be following her. He concentrated on the little red light, as she had ordered him to do, and he thought that his trip to the quarry had consisted of obsessively fixing his eyes on something different, always: first the curb along the avenue, then the tracks of the boys on their way to the little island in the middle of the pond, after that the tracks of the dog that rescued him, and now that red light on the mudguard over this hulking woman's back tire.

He went back to the quarry with his friends in the summer, in what would be their last group excursion because they were tired of riding bikes, they dreamed of getting a motorcycle, the quarry bored them, they'd started going to their first parties and two of them already had girlfriends. When they climbed the gentle slope that positioned them above the large water-filled pit, he could hardly believe what he saw. Without the fog, he thought the place seemed tiny. He thought that maybe it was narrower because that was where the trucks emptied the rubble from the surrounding construction sites, but when he told his friends that the quarry seemed smaller, they disagreed and said it was the same size as it had always been. He hadn't told them about his solitary journey that January afternoon. He himself saw it as something unclear and wondered sometimes if he hadn't dreamed it. They went down the embankment and left their bikes on the grass. There were a few fishermen on the opposite shore. The others sat down to have a cigarette. He couldn't stand tobacco and started walking, trying to figure out where he and the boys had slid across the ice. He was astonished by the proximity of the little island in the middle of the pond. Crossing it in the fog had seemed like a polar excursion, and now, beneath the scorching July sun, it seemed like it would take no more than five minutes. He remembered the wide bubbles detained by the ice on their ascent from the bottom of the pond and it brought back the terror they had caused him. He scrambled up the embankment hoping that from that height he could catch a glimpse of the concrete structure in front of which he had found the man by the fire, but summer, with its tight curtain of trees, obstructed any perspective beyond the perimeter of the mirror of water. Standing at that low height he told himself that his friends were right. It was a boring place, good for a few retired old men who came to cast a fishing line on hot afternoons. He turned back to where his friends were smoking, but he couldn't see them, and he felt the urge to disappear from their lives, their girlfriends and cigarettes. Maybe he still hadn't forgiven them for not wanting to accompany him that January afternoon, when he had climbed on his bike to set out on that summer route in the dead of winter.

Lying on the grass, looking at the sky, he thought that it wouldn't be long before the quarry disappeared. On his winter outing he hadn't noticed it because of the fog, but now summer had revealed that the city was extending its reach all the way to the first farmhouses on the outskirts, absorbing what few farm communities still survived in the suburbs. Maybe that place would be unrecognizable by next winter because they'd cover the quarry to build an office building or shopping center. Then he heard soft footsteps behind him. He recognized the panting and stiffened. He didn't dare turn his head for fear of startling the beast with a sudden movement. The animal's warm breath reached him and he closed his eyes. He was afraid that its sharp ear could hear his heartbeat, and that it wouldn't like that. When he heard it walking away, he remained still for several minutes. It had smelled him and recognized him. He knew, because he'd read John Fillmore's book *A Wolf in Your House* that dogs never forget a scent. Finally he came back to the present. He was dizzy, stood up and walked along the top of the embankment until he reached his friends. When he stopped in front of them and they asked him where he'd gone, he blurted out, "My parents split up."

The four of them looked at one another. One of them asked when, he answered the week before and added that his father no longer lived with them. They looked at one another again. The one who asked when they'd split up took out his pack of cigarettes and offered him one. He shook his head no, but the other insisted. "Don't be a pussy."

He took the cigarette and the others noticed that his fingers were trembling. They each took a cigarette, even though they had each just smoked one. They managed to light all five cigarettes with only one match, and when he started to cough, they laughed at him and showed him how to inhale and blow the smoke out of his nose.

roxie moore

I'd dozed off. When I woke up there were only a few of us left in the room, as well as the blonde in jeans. I rubbed my eyes. I'd slept for about twenty minutes. The blonde was talking about how hard it had been for her to start out in the industry. She said it like that, "industry," instead of "trade" or "profession." I guessed she was about Roxie's age, or no younger than fifty, but she was short and unattractive, so she probably didn't do the same thing as Roxie. There were six of us, including her (I'm talking about the

blonde, not Roxie, who didn't count because she
was dead). I got up to pour myself some coffee from
the machine in the corner of the room, looked at my
watch and saw that I had three hours before I had
to catch my bus back. The blonde was still talking
about her beginnings in the industry, which, she
told us, she'd entered thanks to Roxie. She didn't
call her by name, but said "her." Roxie Moore was
clearly a stage name, and maybe the blonde didn't
want to reveal her friend's real name because she'd
sensed that we were just a few fans. She told us
that they'd met in Los Angeles and she never really
knew where "she" was from, although she thought
she remembered from some place on the East Coast.
In the industry, she said, everyone quickly learns
to hide their original accent, because in front of the
camera one needs to use neutral language. On the
other hand, she added, in this particular genre of
cinema one speaks very little. All five of us smiled,
and she, encouraged by our reaction, said she knew
some actors who bragged about not having uttered
a single word in their entire careers. We laughed
again. Pure moans, she said, and she mimicked
them playfully. She was actually quite pleasant. Of
course, her body was nothing compared to Roxie's,
although she moaned to perfection. Then she told
us that "she," meaning Roxie, had had half of her

left breast removed because of a tumor, which could have been the end of her career, because the plastic surgeon had seriously fucked it up, really fucked it up, and if it hadn't been for her, Roxie would never have set foot on a set again. She asked if any of us had ever noticed the scar on her left breast and another on her belly from an umbilical hernia. The five of us shook our heads. It was evident that none of us who were present, except for the blonde, were relatives or friends of the deceased. I'd swear that the others, like me, had come to say goodbye to Roxie after learning of her death on her website or through some other means. Maybe the same thing happened at all the wakes for every Roxie: Family members, friends, and colleagues depart, and the last ones remaining at the end are the addicted website enthusiasts.

As I said, the five of us shook our heads, and the blonde said that it was of course impossible for us to have noticed anything, despite the fact that both scars were large, because, modesty aside, she knew how to do her job, and if they'd asked her to hide a rhinoceros horn, she would have succeeded at that, too. We smiled again. In this business, she said, there are only two must-haves: erections and makeup. She stood up, walked to the casket, and leaned over Roxie's body; then, addressing the man with glasses, she asked him to keep an eye on the entrance. The man with glasses didn't understand and she told him that he should be on the lookout so no one from the funeral home came in. The guy stood next to the door and we looked at one another hesitantly. Come and see, she said after struggling momentarily with Roxie's body, and we got up and approached the coffin. She'd uncovered Roxie's left boob to show us the scar that ran from her nipple to the underside of her breast. I was stunned, not by the wound but by the exposed boob. I looked at my fellow mourners and saw the same dismay on their faces. I looked at Roxie's face, aged but still beautiful, which until that moment I hadn't dared to look at, content with the photo of her as a young woman, which was placed beside the casket. The funeral-home staff had done a good job hiding the scars from the accident. Look at the difference, the blonde said, uncovering the other boob and rather presumptuously holding both breasts erect. The four of us crammed together to look. I stared at Roxie Moore's Rubenesque breasts, the best breasts on every website specializing in big and mature women. The man wearing the leather jacket stretched out his hand, brushed the scar, and gently squeezed one of her boobs. The one beside me, a chubby bald guy, touched the other one. It was my turn and I palpated both boobs delicately, noting that they retained an enviable firmness despite Roxie's fifty-odd summers. Then the guy with glasses abandoned his post as watchman to come look and the one with the leather jacket took his place at the door. The one with glasses stood there, engrossed, contemplating Roxie, as if he couldn't believe it, and he didn't want to touch her. The blonde unbuttoned the rest of her blouse to show us the scar on her belly. Look at that, she said boastfully. Tell me if it isn't noticeable, and the four of us nodded. Of course the scar was noticeable and there was no doubt the woman knew her job. She moved as if to rebutton the blouse, but the man in the turtleneck sweater grabbed her wrist and told her to wait. He was the oldest in the group, he looked at us, looked at the blonde, and said, Now that you've started, finish it. Finish what? she asked. Taking off her clothes, the old man said. There's nothing else to see, the blonde said, and she tried to pull away, but the old man, who was strong, wouldn't let go. You showed us your work, now we want to see all of her, he said, and then asked the rest of us, What do you say? I kept quiet. Let me go! the blonde said to the old man, but he ignored her and kept looking at us, waiting for an answer. The chubby bald guy said, Yeah, since she started, she should keep going! and the old man looked at me. If we do it, let's make it quick, I said. I'm not going to do anything! the blonde exclaimed. The old man hadn't let go of her hand and he threatened her: Do you want us to call the funeral-home staff and tell them that you uncovered her tits and belly? Did you know that you could end up in jail for something like this? The blonde took a deep breath and must have picked up on our determination; she turned toward the door to make sure that we weren't going to be seen and said, Okay, but let go, you're hurting me. The old man released her and she rubbed her sore wrist. At that, the guy in the leather jacket told us that someone from the funeral home was coming. The old man ordered us to stand shoulder to shoulder in front of the coffin and he started to pray an Our Father. We all followed him in prayer, including the blonde. A short employee came in and when he saw that we were praying he stopped at the door and said something in a low voice to the guy in the leather jacket, then he left and the leather-jacket guy came to tell us that the funeral-home staff would be back in ten minutes to close the casket. Then the guy with glasses, who hadn't opened his mouth until then, said that we weren't going to have time to take off all of Roxie's clothes and that pulling her pants down would be enough. The old man turned to him and shouted in his face, I'm not going to leave her with her pants down! Either we undress her completely or not at all! And he looked at the rest of us, who nodded. Then he motioned to the blonde to help him and between the two of them they lifted Roxie's torso, whose head jostled like a puppet's. The guy in the leather jacket abandoned his lookout post, came over, tapped me on the shoulder, and told me, You go. I was reluctant to do so but I went to stand in the doorway and from there I watched how they removed Roxie's blouse and then took off her pants. I heard a sigh of admiration, couldn't control myself, and went to see her marvelous thighs, but the one in the leather jacket exclaimed, What are you doing? and I had to go back to my sentry post. I then felt that it had always been that way with Roxie: seeing parts of her, in a rush, afraid of being caught. It had been like that at home, in front of the computer, the danger of Edda and the boys coming into the room unexpectedly, and now it was the same at the funeral home, where we could barely brush against her, careful to make sure no one would come in. Roxie, wherever she was, was an unattainable fruit, and perhaps that's why she'd become an obsession. Maybe the old man wanted to see her naked to convince himself that she was just a woman who had earned a living as best as she could. Maybe that's why the five of us were there, next to her coffin.

They started to argue. Like hell I will! the blonde exclaimed, and she came over to me and said that she was taking my place at the door. You are sick, all of you, she said quietly. I walked over to the coffin. The four of them were turning Roxie over. They left her facedown, completely naked, and the chubby one mounded her clothes under her pelvis so that her buttocks were raised up. There was Roxie Moore's formidable ass, the Mecca of all my XXX pilgrimages! Who knows how many hearts had been destroyed by these two white hemispheres, with that maddening ellipse of darkened skin around the junction of the buttocks, a result of a lifetime of rubbing, rubbing like two tectonic plates rubbing together. That was Roxie's indispensable posture, the ultimate nudity one begs for on the web's hardcore sites. That's how I met her and I remember that feeling of being in front of something definitive when I came across her in that quadrupedal position. I had followed her in her gradual aging over the years, but her ass had remained intact and now it was there, just half a meter in front of my eyes, and I bent down to kiss it, first one butt cheek and then the other. The others did the same thing, repeating the same symmetrical kiss, including the man with glasses. Let her go like this, the one in the turtleneck sweater, the oldest of all of us, said then. What do you mean like this? the one in the leather jacket asked. That was Roxie! the old man exclaimed in a rage. At last somebody had pronounced her name. I didn't say anything, because I couldn't take my eyes off her buttocks and I thought the old man was right in way. Roxie had reached her peculiar perfection on all fours and it was only right for her to spend her eternal rest facedown. The old man pulled out a hundred-dollar bill, showed it to us, and said, We'll settle up later. A minute later a young man from the funeral home appeared with a screwdriver in his hand. The old man called him over, we made room for him next to the casket and when he saw Roxie in the buff and facedown, he looked on in astonishment. He was just a youngster. It is our wish and once you close the casket, no one is going to find out, the old man told him, showing him the hundred-dollar bill. He slipped it into his shirt pocket and gave it three taps to close the deal. The young man looked at us, he was scared, gulped, and proceeded to close the casket. We respectfully took a step back, watched how he tightened the bolts on the lid, and we sat back down. Soon after another employee came in, pushing a metal frame on wheels. Between the two of them, they loaded the casket onto the frame and took it away. Then the old man stood up to ask for twenty dollars from each of us. When the blonde made the gesture to open her purse, he signaled that there was no need. It's on us, he told her, and the rest of us nodded our heads in approval.

night bakery

During my time in Berlin I just walked around and didn't read a single book. In a way I replaced reading with walking. My first walk was at 5:40 a.m. to buy the bread. There was a bakery in front of my house, but their bread was pretty bad, so I looked for and found another one, a ways away, that sold excellent bread and opened at six. I usually write early so I'd go out at 5:40 to be at the bakery right at six, buy the *acht kleine Bröchten*, which was the daily amount of bread we ate at home, and then I

returned to write. I did this both in winter, long before dawn, eight or ten degrees below zero, and in
summer, when at 5:40 the upper-floor windows of
the surrounding buildings were already glimmer-
ing with the first rays of sunlight.

I've always enjoyed walking very early in the
morning, still night, when signs of the new day
begin to appear and the first building windows
light up. Sometimes a solitary woman would cross
my path and I was pleased to see that she felt safe
meeting me, because something in the way I walked
conveyed that she had nothing to fear. A brief look
a few meters before we were face-to-face, sometimes
accompanied with a smile, reaffirmed her safety.

On the way back from the bakery my appearance was not only reassuring but even insignificant.
What can be dangerous about a man carrying a bag
of bread under his arm? The women who passed
me no longer wasted a smile on me or even looked
me in the eye, wrapped as they were in the rhythm
of the waking city. In hardly ten minutes the same
Berlin as usual had been born, where no one looks
at anyone else.

Despite arriving promptly at six, every morning
I encountered a customer at the bakery who'd arrived earlier than me. A man between fifty and sixty
years old. He ate breakfast standing up, a cup of

coffee and croissant, reading the newspaper spread across the only table in the establishment. He was always there, engrossed in what he was reading, and he never turned to look at me, so I could never see his face. Maybe that's why I decided to go earlier one morning, and I left ten minutes before I usually did, at half past five, and I arrived at the bakery at ten to six. To my surprise, it was already open and the guy was inside, eating his croissant and reading the newspaper. On my way out, I checked the schedule posted on the door, which clearly stated that the small shop opened at six o'clock. A German sign, to someone not German, has the likeness of a military bulletin and cannot lie. If the opening time was six o'clock, why was the bakery already open at 5:50?

The next day I went even earlier and arrived at half past five. Of all my walks it was the one I enjoyed the least because I was almost running. I saw from a distance the illuminated bakery. When I entered, the croissant man was already immersed in his newspaper, while the baker busied himself with something. I was about to ask him what time they really opened, but my limited German didn't allow for clarifications or questions. Over the following days I stopped worrying about unseating the guy from his dreary first place, which maybe he won because he suffered from fierce insomnia, and I imagined a story in which that situation was stretched to the point of absurdity: The bakery never closed, and the mysterious customer was there, with his croissant and reading the newspaper, like a Hopper painting stopped forever.

In fact, he may still be there, reading his newspaper every morning and standing at the same table. After all these years I'm still wondering where he was getting the newspaper so early, if none of the paper stands opened before six. Did he read the previous day's newspaper? And only now do I arrive at the conclusion that he was probably the owner of the bakery; that's why he was the first to arrive and will always arrive first. Why didn't I think of that before?

Maybe if the events that I am recounting had occurred in broad daylight, the man wouldn't have become a curiosity, but in that stealthy hour when a city is on the verge of waking, his presence in the bakery wound up symbolizing the precarious situation of those of us who write, always condemned to have far fewer readers than we think we deserve. The man was the representation of the unattainable reader, the one who was never going to be touched by my words because others absorbed him, certainly more urgent, deeper, and more necessary than mine.

Nothing about me, not my foreign accent, not the tone of my voice, not my style of speaking, managed to distract him for a single moment, and I'm sure, if he registered my presence, he would forget it as soon as I walked out of the bakery.

During my time in Berlin, where I'd gone to take care of my sister Karla, I didn't read a single book and, contrary to my habit, I walked very little, because caring for my sick sister kept me busy all day. I couldn't find the time or the desire to immerse myself in a book so I had to limit myself to reading the newspaper, one from the previous day no less, because my only free moments were early in the morning, before Karla woke up, and at that time the newspaper stands are closed. It wasn't something that affected me because I'm not in the habit of reading the papers. Besides, more than reading the newspaper, I immersed myself in it to escape from the city that surrounded me, because I abhor Berlin, that gray and sprawling, noisy and crowded city, where it's impossible to walk. I've never understood why Karla, after the death of her husband, Moritz, wanted to stay there.

There was a bakery across the street from Karla's house. They made a poor-quality bread, just like every other bakery in Berlin, but it was steps away: I'd cross the street and was inside. I could have gone in my pajamas because there wasn't a soul on the street at that hour. Besides, since Heinrich, the owner, was an old friend of Karla's (he even owed her money), I could go down to his shop before six, which was when it opened, when Uwe, the attendant, and Sabine, his wife, were just beginning to fill the shelves with the bread that a van delivered to them. Sabine, as soon as she saw me crossing the street, started to prepare my coffee with milk and would put a croissant in the electric oven to warm it up. I was, in essence, their first customer, an anomalous customer, a kind of family friend they served before opening hours. For this reason, as long as I was around, the bakery wound up having flexible opening hours because, with me inside, Uwe and Sabine would leave the door open and anyone could enter before six.

I remember a man, one whose face I never saw, a foreigner, probably Latin American, who arrived every morning before anyone else and always asked for the same thing, like some cantilena he'd memorized: *"Acht kleine Bröchten."* I knew he was a Spanish-speaker because Uwe, who had no sympathy for foreigners, asked him a malicious question one day, just to find out how much German he understood: "How do you calculate the volume of a polygon?" A stupid question, to which the other answered in Spanish, "*Perdone?*" and Uwe said, also in Spanish, "*Nada, nada,*" and handed him the bag with his eight pieces of bread. He was upset because the guy had entered the bakery at 5:50, ten minutes before the sign on the door said they opened, and said to Sabine, "Those third worlders don't even know how to read numbers." I avoided their glances because I knew that it was my fault they had to attend to customers before six o'clock. But why didn't they close the door if it bothered them? I told Karla about the episode, and she, who knew Uwe and his wife well, told me that by closing the door to the bakery they would have created a kind of intimacy between them and me; in short, they would have felt obliged to speak to me, so they preferred to leave the door open and serve any absent-minded customers who came in before opening time. I believed her, because Berliners are like that, incapable of carrying on a conversation for the simple pleasure of talking. In my town, on the other hand...but I don't want to talk about my town. I accepted my sister's explanation and stopped worrying about it. However, the next morning the clueless guy arrived

even earlier: at half past five. I had just situated myself at the little table in the corner, facing the wall,
when I heard that cantilena behind me, *"Acht kleine
Bröchten,"* and plunged my head into the newspaper, imagining Uwe's rage. I couldn't concentrate
on what I was reading and left a larger than usual
tip on the table. I didn't say anything to Karla, but
that night I could barely sleep. I was afraid that
the man would arrive at the bakery earlier the next
day, even earlier than me, forcing Uwe and Sabine
to gather the eight pieces of bread he was buying
directly from the van, an effort that I'd have to com-
pensate for by leaving an even bigger tip than the
one I'd already left. I could already see the bitter
look on Uwe's face watching me cross the street and
Sabine's coolness as she served me my croissant and
coffee with milk, and I almost didn't go down to the
bakery. But I didn't have any other place to have
breakfast and, fortunately, the man arrived at six
on the dot and from then on he never arrived before
that time. Every morning I waited for him to arrive,
and although I was tempted to turn my head several
times, I never did, obeying I don't know what personal prohibition.

"Acht kleine Bröchten." These words, spoken with
a foreign accent, now that Karla has died and I've
returned to my town, come to mind when I least

expect it. I'm reading books again, walking, and, as is my habit, I don't read any newspapers. I'll never go back to Berlin again. I barely remember the faces of Uwe and Sabine. The truth is I never really looked at their faces. I feel like I was turning my back on everyone and everything during the time I lived in Berlin, while praying that Karla wouldn't die, and that the only thing I hold on to from that trip are those three words spoken by a stranger.

the bonfire

He approached with his book in his hand, asked permission to sit down, and the boys made room for him near the fire.

"It's nice and warm!" he said, setting the book on the sand and rubbing his hands together with satisfaction.

He looked at the backpacks the teens had piled to one side of the bonfire. All of them were designer brands, just as his expert eye had detected that afternoon when he saw them getting off the bus.

He thought that the fire wasn't going to last long, because they hadn't taken care to dig a hole to protect the flames from the wind. He stood up and said, "I'm going to get some firewood." And he headed toward some palm trees about a hundred meters away, where the beach formed a wide depression. There were several branches, though they were still damp from the rain that afternoon. He gathered the driest ones, returned to the bonfire, and dropped the bundle to one side of the backpacks, because he wanted to make sure they didn't have locks on them. He didn't see any. He started to feed the fire with the branches and thought that if he didn't get some thicker and drier wood, the fire would die out and the snotty brats might leave. He remembered a eucalyptus log he'd seen near the mouth of the creek. A log only gets wet on the outside and, if the fire is tended carefully, it can last all night. He walked to the creek, the log was still there, and then went back to the boys to tell them that he needed someone to help him carry it back. They started teasing one another to see who would go with him, and in the end it was all just pushing and shoving and laughter and nobody got up. Slackers, he thought, going back to his place by the fire, and when they started to throw pieces of wood at each other, laughing wildly, he tried to laugh with them so they'd like him. It was at that moment that a tall woman with glasses, Nordic-looking, emerged from the darkness. She had a cigarette in her hand and walked over to ask them for a light.

"Who has a lighter?" one of the teens asked.

"No need," he said, and lifting a branch out of the fire he offered the burning tip to the woman, who leaned in with the cigarette in her mouth and drew in several puffs to light it. He estimated her to be between forty and fifty years old, the classic older European woman who comes in search of a tan and, if possible, some romance, but above all, fleeing from the cold.

She let out a puff of smoke, looked at the bonfire, and said with a strong foreign accent, "It's going to die out."

"There's no more wood," one of the boys said.

"We should go to one of those," the one beside him said, pointing at a few bonfires that could be seen at the other end of the beach.

He, in a last attempt to stoke the fire, put his book on the sand, pulled off the cardboard cover, and brought it close to the flames, causing a flame to leap up and hold the slackers spellbound. Then he ripped the back cover off the book and threw it onto the bonfire, along with a few pages. The woman shouted, "What are you doing? You don't burn books," and, throwing down her cigarette, she knelt by the fire, removed as best as she could the pages that were beginning to burn and blew on them to extinguish the embers. Then, standing up, she asked him to give her the book. He obeyed, impressed by her boldness. With the book in her hand, she walked away, tall and lanky, and sat near the seashore. There was laughter around the circle of boys and he thought they were laughing because he had obeyed the woman without talking back to her. He stood up and walked toward her; she had lined up the singed pages on the sand and was trying to put them in order.

"Give me back my book," he said.

"I'm putting the pages in order."

"There's no need to put them in order, I'm not going to read it."

"You were going to burn a book that you haven't even read!" she said, shaking her head.

"A fire's more important than a book," he said.

"A fire's more important than a book!" the woman repeated, as if she thought it were an inhuman sentence. "Do you think it's easy to write one?"

"It isn't easy to build a fire and keep it going all night," he exclaimed, pointing to the bonfire, and turning his head he saw that the teens were picking up their backpacks. When the fire went out, they'd lost interest in staying there, or perhaps they were taking advantage of this mishap to get rid of his company because they had suspected something. He knew that they were heading to the other end of the beach, attracted by the other fires. That was forbidden territory for him and he couldn't follow them.

He watched them leave, replied to their wave by raising his arm, and then he looked back at her. "You see? They left," he said.

"Aren't they friends of yours?"

"Those brats? No."

She gathered the pages she had put in order and handed them back to him along with the book, but he wouldn't take it.

"You can keep it, it's no good to me like that," he said.

"You threw it into the fire."

"Right, so that those brats wouldn't leave! I've had my eye on them since they got off the bus this afternoon. High-end designer backpacks. Carrying a book always helps."

"Helps with what?" She had stood up and he looked at her, but in the darkness he could only see the reflection of her glasses.

"Lady, you're not as smart as you think," he said. She wasn't so old, after all, that he had to address her formally. "You probably read a lot of books, but you're not as smart as you think you are."

She moved as if she were about to leave, but he stepped in front of her, almost pressing his face to hers, to the point he could feel her breath. She looked in the direction of the boys who had just left. She was frightened, and he felt a little ashamed because the woman was twice his age, but he couldn't back down, and raising his voice, he criticized her: "I was winning them over and you ruined everything because you wanted to save this stupid book!"

He hit her hand inadvertently and the book fell to the ground. The singed pages scattered across the sand. She hesitated a moment, then knelt down to pick them up. He watched her stretch her full length when a page slipped out of her of hands; on her knees, she gathered all the pages around her and made a bundle she put between the pages of the book so the wind wouldn't blow them away.

"You're missing that one," he said, pointing to a page behind her. She turned her head and grabbed it. She was breathing heavily.

"Does this book matter so much to you?"

"It's a book," she said. "Take it." And she held out her arm to give it to him.

"I already told you I'm not going to read it."

A large wave slid up to where they were, came in strong and tossed the woman sideways; she screamed in surprise, still holding the book, so it wouldn't get wet.

"Give it to me!" he said, taking two steps toward her, and he felt the water seep into his leather boots and fill them with sand. He let out a "Fuck!" and, with the book in his hand, he walked away from the water.

"What a wave!" she exclaimed, still on her knees. She was soaked from head to toe and laughing.

He went to sit down where the sand wasn't wet, put the book aside, and tried to pull off his boots. He managed to remove one after some effort and turned it upside down to get the sludge out. A gust of air blew the book open, one of the pages flew out, he stood up and, hobbling after it wearing a single boot, tried to grab it. Another gust scattered the rest of the pages, they began to come loose one by one, flying in all directions, and he gave up chasing them.

"Everything's ruined," he said, and looked at her; she hadn't moved and was wringing out her wet hair. Some of the pages had ended their journey on the backwash, which was now carrying them out to sea.

He sat back down on the sand to remove his other boot. He tried but couldn't. "If those fools had been more enthusiastic, we'd have a fire going all night and I could dry my boots," he said. "Bunch of slackers! I don't like people who don't apply themselves."

"How do you apply yourself?" she asked him. "Robbing snotty brats?"

"I work in a sawmill, okay? That thing with the kids happens from time to time, if the opportunity presents itself. I bought these boots, which cost me an arm and a leg, and now the seawater is going to ruin them."

He tried to remove his boot again, but it refused to come off. He lay back on the sand faceup, worn out, and thought that if she wanted to escape, now was the time. He, wearing just one boot, wouldn't be able to catch her. He had absolutely no intention of running after her, but she didn't know that, and maybe she was waiting for the chance to slip away. He felt her grab his foot, he straightened up and saw that she was holding his boot by the heel. "What are you doing?"

"Pull toward yourself."

He obeyed, they struggled for a while and finally between the two of them managed to free his foot. He took off his sock and rubbed his sore foot. She was panting from the effort, and her face, which he had noted only briefly, was now etched in his memory once and for all, despite the darkness. He had the urge to ask her what her name was. Instead he said, "There's a eucalyptus log. If you help me carry it, we can start a fire to dry my boots and your clothes."

"Where?"

"Next to the creek," and he pointed to the place behind them. He tucked his socks into his boots and stood up. "Are you coming?"

She stood up and touched her soaked shorts and T-shirt, looked one last time at what was left of the book, picked up her sandals, and walked behind him.

oncologist

The Friday he returned from a birthday party for
Elisa, the director of the Department of Radiogra-
phy at the hospital where he worked, Luis realized
that he didn't have his keys with him. He'd had a lot
to drink and at some point he'd most likely dropped
them by mistake. It was two o'clock in the morning and there was no one at home. Natalia, his wife,
had gone to Monterrey to see her brother, and their
daughter was on a school trip. He had no choice but
to wake up Marilú, their neighbor, who lived in one

of the building's two penthouses. At one point, after having lost her keys, Marilú had asked him and Natalia to keep a set for her, in case it happened again, and they in turn had given her a copy of theirs. Luis hesitated a little before calling her, but in the end he told himself that the agreement they had with her was for emergencies of this kind. When Marilú answered, he could hear, along with her voice, the sound of a cumbia, and breathed a sigh of relief, realizing that she was still awake. He told her that he had lost his keys and asked her to forgive him for disturbing her at that hour. She told him that she was having a party in her apartment, so it was no bother, and buzzed him in through the front gate.

As he rode up in the elevator the sound of the music grew louder and louder, and when he reached the top floor the door to the penthouse was open and he thought that Marilú had left it that way so he could go in. Nevertheless, he preferred to wait on the landing. The large apartment was almost completely dark and he could see that there were people dancing. It was an all-out bash, not just a simple party, and he appreciated the fact that he lived three floors down and in the opposite wing of the building, where the clamor of music couldn't be heard. Seeing that Marilú wasn't going to show up, he went inside and closed the door behind him. He

looked for her in the semidarkness, didn't see her
and went out to the terrace, where more people were
gathered. She wasn't there either. He approached
the railing and watched the flow of cars on the beltway. It was incredible that there was still traffic at
that hour. He'd never been in Marilú's penthouse
before. His friendship with her had developed on
the stair landings and when they saw each other in
the elevator.

He went back to the living room and, since he
didn't see her, assumed that she must have been in
one of the bedrooms. He walked over to the bar, the
only part of the apartment that was fairly well lit,
and ordered a Cuba libre from the bartender, who
was dressed in white. He saw a small sofa next to
the picture window looking onto the terrace and
went to sit there with his glass. It was a good place,
because he could see both the terrace and the living
room at the same time. He observed the guests and
it was then that he saw her in a corner. She was
dancing with a tall man who seemed to be a bit
older than her. Dancing, in a manner of speaking.
They were almost motionless, clutching each other
in a way that left no doubt about the type of relationship they had. Marilú's head rested on the man's
chest, and he stroked her hair. He watched them,
hoping she would turn around and see him. He was

beginning to feel anxious that she'd forgotten about him. He finished his Cuba and it dawned on him that he was going to have to wait a while before getting his keys. He got up to get another, and as he stood up, he saw the piece of paper, partially hidden between the two seat cushions of the sofa he was sitting on. He picked it up to see what was on it and recognized the seal of a clinical analysis laboratory. He tilted the paper so that the light coming in from the terrace would help him read it. It was a pancreas biopsy. He saw that it was the second sheet; the first, with the patient information, was missing. He immediately looked for the direct bilirubin panels. Seeing that the index was well outside the usual range, he sat down again and brought the paper closer to his face so he could make out the date. It was from that same day, and it gave the time: 8:52 in the morning. Seeing that no one was looking at him, he folded the sheet and put it in the outer pocket of his jacket. His heart was pounding, and he sat there for a while without moving with the empty glass in his hand. Someone, perhaps one of the guests at the party, had advanced pancreatic cancer. He looked around for Marilú. She was still in the corner, in the arms of the tall man. Perhaps the analyses were hers and the man held her in a comforting embrace. Or it was the other way around, and she consoled him.

He stood up, went to the bar, and ordered another Cuba libre, then he went out to the terrace and leaned against the railing to protect himself from the wind. He watched the flow of cars on the beltway. He had put the paper in his pocket without thinking about it; it was an instinctive reflex. Certain results shouldn't be left on display for everyone to see. Now the paper weighed him down. He thought about throwing it off the terrace, after wadding it into a ball inside his pocket, but he dismissed the idea because its owner was most likely looking for it. He looked at the people around him. Those who weren't dancing talked comfortably and no one seemed to have the appearance of someone who'd just received the news that they only had a few months to live. An advanced-stage pancreatic tumor can produce a yellowish color in the skin and whites of the eyes, but he would have needed more light to recognize those indications in the people around him.

He started to feel cold, returned to the living room, and looked in Marilú's direction. She and the tall man were still glued together, and they were hardly moving. He couldn't ask for his keys while they were nuzzling like that. When he could finally do so, he would take her aside and show her the page he had found on the sofa. He imagined Marilú telling him in a low voice, "Yes, Luis, it's my analysis, I took them out with the sole intention of showing them to you."

He saw that the couple who had been on the sofa had stood up to dance and he went back to sit there. He thought it might be best to leave the page where he'd found it. He felt slightly dizzy and rested his head on the backrest. He was afraid that some women might approach him and ask him to dance. He didn't like to dance and, above all, he hated salsa music. He closed his eyes, and shortly after someone tapped him on the shoulder. A tall woman was looking at him and asked him something he didn't understand.

"No, thank you, I'd rather not dance," Luis said.

"Me neither. Can you stand up for a moment, please?"

He stood up. The woman lifted the sofa cushion, looked under it, and lifted the other cushion. Luis asked her if she'd lost something.

"Yes, but maybe not here," she said, putting the cushions back. She apologized and asked him to sit down again, then she sat down, clutching her purse to her chest, and he thought that she was the only woman at the party who was carrying a purse, as if she were about to leave.

"Is it something important?" he asked.

"Yes," the woman replied.

He looked at her eyes. They weren't yellow and her skin looked healthy, but it wasn't a decisive indication, and he would have needed more light to be sure. He took the sheet of paper out of his pocket. "Is this what you are looking for?"

She took the page, looked at it, and said, "Yes, where did you find it?"

"Here." He pointed at the sofa where they were sitting. The woman thanked him and opened her purse and put the paper inside.

"I'm an oncologist," Luis said, as if to justify putting the page in his pocket, and she turned her head abruptly to look at him. "It's a carcinoma and one doesn't just leave analyses like these on a sofa, at a party, as if it were nothing. That's why I picked them up."

"I understand," she said.

He took a swig of his Cuba and asked his question in an uncertain voice, "Are they yours?"

"The analyses?" she said.

"Yes."

"No, a friend's."

"And the doctor has already seen them?"

"I beg your pardon?"

"If your friend's doctor has already seen them."

"I'm her doctor," she said.

"Ah, we're colleagues," he exclaimed, relieved, and took another drink of his Cuba.

"Internist," she clarified. "But in this case it's your opinion that counts." And she looked at him, as if waiting for his opinion. Luis swallowed the last of his Cuba.

"It's a stage-three carcinoma, the most advanced," he said.

She nodded slowly and looked at the floor. She looked up at him again to ask, "How much time would you say?"

"One year, at most. How old?"

"Who?"

"Your friend."

"My age."

He observed her and again took notice of her skin and eyes. It was too dark to see. He pulled out his pack of cigarettes and offered her one. She made a gesture of refusal and he put the pack back in his pocket. It had occurred to him that he might get a closer look at her eyes when he raised the lighter to her cigarette. "Are you a friend of Marilú's?" he asked.

"No, I'm a friend of the next-door neighbor. I came to see her, but she wasn't there." She ran a hand through her hair and hesitated for a moment before adding: "When I saw the door open and heard the music, I thought she might be here and that inspired

me to come in, but she isn't here. I don't know anyone, not even the owner of the place."

"Is she the friend who...?" Luis pointed at the
page of analyses that she had just put in her purse.

"Yes," the woman replied.

"I'm also a kind of party-crasher," he said. "I
don't know anyone, except Marilú."

"Could you bring me a Cuba?" she said.

"Of course." He stood up. "That way I can get
another one." He walked over to the bar and ordered the two drinks. While the bartender prepared them he couldn't help looking at the color of
his eyes and skin.

When he returned to the sofa she was gone. He
didn't see her among those who were dancing and
went out to the terrace holding the two glasses.
They'd also started to dance out there. He moved
slowly, careful not to spill the drinks. Maybe she'd
gone to the bathroom. He went back to the sofa to
wait for her, but the couple from before had returned
to occupy it, so he looked for a place to set the woman's Cuba, returned to the bar, and left the drink on it.

"Something wrong with the drink?" the bartender asked.

"No, I can't find the person who asked me for it."
And he asked him if he hadn't seen a tall, middle-
aged woman leave the apartment.

"I didn't notice," the man answered.

He looked for her again among the dancers and realized that he could barely remember her face. He had been looking at her profile the whole time and had observed her eyes but not her face. He wouldn't have been able to say whether she was a beautiful woman. He walked around the terrace again and went up to the railing. The beltway was almost empty. He saw a white car parked on the street, its engine had just started and the lights came on, ready to leave. It was parked badly, as if its owner had pulled in with the intention of staying as little time as possible. He swore it was her. The car pulled out and drove away, until he lost sight of it. He thought that if she had really gone to her friend's house to show her the test results, like she'd said, she wouldn't have parked like that. She'd lied to him. She was at that party to show the analysis to her doctor, who had told her to go there because she didn't want to wait until Monday to find out about the results of her biopsy. She'd waited for him in that unfamiliar apartment, perhaps to no avail, and, about to leave, she had realized she'd lost the page with the results. Learning that he was an oncologist, she'd told him that she was also a doctor, so that he wouldn't suspect that the analyses were hers.

He turned his head. Someone had touched his shoulder. Marilú was looking at him with a smirk, swinging his keys in front of his face. Her eyes weren't yellowish and her skin looked normal, but that wasn't a decisive indication.

"I'll give them to you on one condition," she told him. She looked drunk, although she concealed it well. He thought she was going to ask him to return the page with the analyses on it, because someone had seen him put it in his jacket pocket.

"What is it?" he asked.

"Dance with me." And she began to twist and weave to the rhythm of the music.

Luis placed his Cuba on the railing, ready to indulge her, as long as she gave him his keys. But before that he asked her who lived in the apartment next door.

"No one. It's been empty for a year."

He opened his mouth and stared at her.

"Why? Is something wrong?" the owner of the apartment asked.

"No," he answered mechanically.

Marilú dangled the keys in front of him mockingly and he began to move, even though he hated salsa.

the balcony

Josué, his four-year-old cousin, ran down the long balcony to where he waited at the other end with open arms to hug him against his chest. The little one would gleefully squirm out of his embrace and run back to the other end of the balcony to do it again. Suddenly, at the moment his cousin stretched out his little arms, he moved to one side to play a joke on him, the little boy couldn't stop and hit his face against the bars of the railing. He didn't cry right away, but a few seconds later, and his mother, who was in the kitchen, came out to see what was going on. His forehead had wedged between the bars and she pulled him out gently to keep from hurting him. He, frightened by what he had done, said nothing and his aunt didn't ask him anything either, didn't even look at him, as if she had surmised everything; she picked up her son and carried him back into the kitchen, leaving him alone on the balcony. A few neighbors who had leaned out of their windows when they heard the little boy's screams now looked at him, perhaps suspecting what had happened.

Soon after that his aunt, who had just been widowed, moved to the country, and he stopped seeing them. Many years later, after his parents died, one shortly after the other, he traveled to Mexico, attracted by its beaches and Mayan ruins. The trip turned into a longer stay for his studies, which turned into a job that, in spite of the lousy pay, allowed him to travel throughout the country. When he was offered a position of responsibility in a small aluminum-profile company, with the possibility of becoming a partner, he had already been in Mexico for seven years and began to seriously doubt that he would go back to his country.

The news of his aunt's death, which Josué had conveyed to him in a terse e-mail, made him feel even more detached from his homeland. It was from there that he began to remember what had happened that morning. He saw his cousin's little head, wedged between the balcony railing, and the thought that he could have passed between the bars from the momentum of his run, propelling his body forward into a seven-story fall, chilled his blood and sometimes woke him up at night.

One day, eating lunch with two friends, he brought up the incident out of the blue. He told the story hurriedly, omitting several details, and when he finished, his friends nodded distractedly and went back to the subject they had been discussing. That indifference hurt him, and for the first time since he had been living in Mexico he wondered if the time hadn't come for him to return to his country. However, one of them called that night to tell him that he knew very well how he felt, because sometimes he also woke up at night, haunted by the memory of some nefarious act he'd committed in the past. What had happened with his cousin, he added, was terrible, but he shouldn't live overwhelmed with guilt. He thanked him for calling and they said goodbye. However, after hanging up, he had the feeling that they had been talking about two different events. His friend had used the adjective "terrible," and he wondered what he had understood. Did he think that Josué had fallen from the balcony? He dialed his number to clarify things, but the phone was busy; he tried again, to no avail, and when he picked up the handset for the third time, he wasn't sure if he should call or not. Finally, he didn't, and he thought that all he needed to do was let the story go its own way. Far from his country, who was going to contradict this? His decision to settle abroad would take on, in the eyes of those who knew him, new meaning. Especially for Silvia, whom he had not seen since they'd broken up; when she found out about that unfortunate event in his adolescence, she'd see him in a different light.

From that day forward he had the feeling that in the meetings and meals he attended, everyone's attention was focused on him and that an expectant silence surrounded him when he opened his mouth. Had that rumor spread among his acquaintances? He did nothing to find out, resigning himself to the cautious tone it seemed his friends and colleagues used with him now. He felt like he was again surrounded by a certain aura, the same aura that upon his arrival in Mexico had earned him foreign status and that, because he had integrated into local life, had slowly been fading. However, that memory never stopped assaulting him wherever he was. He clenched his fists and jaw at the movies, in bed, or in the middle of a meeting at work. Now more

than ever he mourned the death of his aunt. She
was the only person who would have been able to
offer her insight into the event, and also the only
one who could have forgiven him. He couldn't get
her reaction on the balcony out of his head: not one
question, not a word of reproach, not even a glance.
He felt that she had expressed her contempt for him
through her silence, and that was the most painful
part of the memory.

Then, one morning, while he was preparing a
cup of coffee, it occurred to him to write Josué and
invite him to Mexico. In the same e-mail where he
had reported the death of his mother, his cousin had
informed him of his recent divorce, and he thought
it would be a nice gesture on his part to offer his
house during such a difficult time.

He wondered if he would remember the balcony
incident. Probably not, unless his mother had reminded him. Perhaps, by inviting him, that episode
would take on its appropriate dimensions and he
would stop obsessing over it.

He wrote him that same afternoon and Josué
answered immediately. He had never been to Mexico and, after the failure of his marriage, a vacation
would do him good. His memory of the adorable boy
with whom he had played during so many afternoons
of his adolescence was fuzzy and he was curious to

see what kind of person the only true relative he had left had become. When he went to the airport to meet him, they had no problem recognizing each other. Blessed familiarity of our blood! Josué's effusive embrace melted his fears and, during the car ride from the airport to the house, everything that had happened on the balcony seemed like an insignificant episode, which he could swear his cousin didn't remember at all. However, at one point when Josué ran a hand through his hair, he noticed a scar on his forehead. He bit his lip and asked him what had happened.

"I didn't even remember that I had it," Josué said, touching his scar.

"You don't remember how you got it?"

"No, why?"

"Nothing, it just caught my attention."

He didn't introduce him to his friends right away. First, he wanted to show him the capital. It had been a long time since he had ventured out of the two or three comfortable neighborhoods that made up his safety zone, and he discovered how deeply unfamiliar he was with the rest of the city. He had always boasted about not having the qualms and prejudices of the foreigners who made their home there, but now, in the face of so many sweeping changes, it occurred to him that the reality of that country had escaped him and he felt once again as strange as on the day he arrived, something he tried to hide from his cousin because he wanted to show him that he had succeeded in making that setting his new homeland.

He learned how much his aunt had loved him on those trips.

"She always worshiped you, cousin. She talked more about you than my father," Josué told him.

"But I'm sure she complained about something I did, didn't she?"

"Complain? My God, she only praised you! Your cousin Bernardo this and your cousin Bernardo that. I knew the tune by heart, and when she started up, I stopped listening."

He was tempted to mention the balcony incident, but he didn't, afraid his cousin would have the same reaction of indifference his two friends had in the restaurant. His presence was enough to reduce that event to an inconsequential occurrence, and he felt so good having him around that he suggested that he stay longer than the ten days that he had planned.

"I hardly brought anything, cousin, only three pairs of clothes," Josué said.

"I have plenty of clothes and we're the same size, you won't even have to buy socks."

Josué allowed himself to be convinced. Fresh from his divorce, not tied down to any particular place, in that he was a translator and could work from home, he agreed to stay the whole month. He planned a gathering so he could meet his friends, and because Josué was young, kind, and handsome, everyone liked him. They began to go out together, and it seemed to him that, now that Josué was with him, people invited him out more than before. Not long after, when he said that an audit of his business would keep him fully absorbed for the next two weeks, Josué had no problem going out on his own. He already moved freely among his circle of friends, as if they had always known him. The charm of youth! he said to himself, still feeling slightly jealous.

He was afraid that that abominable rumor, which he had allowed to spread in a moment of obfuscation, would find its way to his cousin's ears. He had prepared a speech to convince him that his words had been twisted. However, Josué never mentioned any of that to him. He concluded that there had never been such a rumor; it had all been a figment of his imagination based on simple gestures and glances. Most likely, he told himself, the friend who had described the event as terrible no longer remembered it; perhaps he had forgotten it at the very moment he hung up the phone, and again he felt that this was the fate of foreigners in that country: They were enveloped in either a luminous aura or one of indifference, with no middle ground, and he wondered which was his.

When he learned that Silvia had returned from her trip to the United States, he fantasized about an encounter between her and his cousin, and wondered if that wasn't why he had invited Josué to Mexico: so he and Silvia could get to know each other, or to put it another way, so that all his friends—but Silvia, above all—might, through his cousin, see him more fully, just as he was, with that transparency that comes about only in the presence of a close relative.

The opportunity arose when a friend organized a dinner to which he knew Silvia would be invited; he pretended to get sick and, as usual, he asked Josué to go in his place. That night, lying in bed, he awaited his cousin's return like an apprehensive mother. As the hours passed, and Josué hadn't returned, he was racked with jealousy. He could see Silvia back him into a corner to make small talk, offer to give him a ride in her car after dinner and then invite him to her apartment for a drink. Before dawn the apartment door opened and he heard his cousin come in, accompanied by a woman. He got up and walked to the door to listen. His heart was pounding, he could hear them talking in a low voice but he couldn't recognize the woman's voice. He wondered if Silvia would be capable of humiliating him like that, sleeping with his cousin in his own house. He heard that they closed the door to Josué's room and he dialed Silvia's house from his cell phone. She answered in a sleepy voice. He hung up in relief and went back to bed.

The next day he left home early to avoid seeing Josué and his friend. That evening, back from the office, his cousin asked him if he'd woken him up the previous night.

"No, why?"

"I made some noise. I wasn't alone."

"Who were you with?"

"With Lucero."

"Silvia Agamben's cousin?"

"Yes. She drove me back in her car after dinner and slept here. It won't happen again, cousin."

"Damn, Josué, I'm not as namby-pamby as you think."

"No, you don't understand, I'm leaving. I bought my ticket back this morning. I leave on Wednesday."

"Are you kidding?"

"No, I've already bothered you enough. I planned to be here for ten days and I've been here almost two months."

"You haven't bothered me in the least, Josué! Exactly the opposite."

"I've had a great time, but I need to go." They were drinking whiskey, Josué took a sip from his glass and added, "It also has to do with Lucero."

"Have you been seeing her?"

"Yes."

"Why didn't you tell me?"

"She told me about you and Silvia, and since you never said anything to me about it, I thought you didn't want me to know, so I decided not to tell you that I was going out with her cousin."

So aptly had it come out, he thought Josué had prepared that sentence beforehand.

"The truth is that I never wanted to hide what happened between me and Silvia from you," he said. "It's just not something I like to talk about."

"I know."

"What do you know?"

"That the thing between you two ended badly, cousin."

"Lucero told you that?"

"She said a little and Silvia a little."

"When did you talk to Silvia?"

"Yesterday." Josué took a swig of his whiskey. "Lucero was taking a shower and Silvia told me about you."

"What did she tell you?"

"That she's never loved another man as much as you."

"But now she hates me."

"She doesn't hate you, but she says that you're incapable of love."

He felt despair flood into his core. He took a sip of whiskey to hide it and his cousin continued, "She told me that you're afraid of hurting others, of suddenly doing something monstrous or inappropriate, and because of that you prefer not to love anyone."

He wondered if she had used the words "inappropriate" and "monstrous," or whether they were his cousin's handiwork.

"I thought she hated me," he said, and added, "I've been stupid."

"Who isn't?"

"Stay, don't be afraid to love Lucero, so you don't regret it like I do."

"No, I know myself," Josué said. "I start out running and everything seems wonderful, then, all of a sudden, I notice a void, as if someone has pulled a rug out from under my feet or I've crashed into something."

He looked at his cousin. He felt certain that he remembered nothing of that distant morning when he had betrayed his trust, stepping aside the moment he had reached his hands out to embrace him. He wondered if that joke had turned him into a surly animal, afraid of the slightest blow that could hurt him. No, it was absurd that an entire life could be dependent upon on such a banal mishap. The man beside him had very little to do with the child from that remote morning. That's why it was absurd to ask for forgiveness; only that boy could forgive him; in fact, he had forgiven him; he remembered that after his mother had rubbed alcohol on his forehead, they had gone back to playing in Josué's room, as if nothing had happened. His mistake had been to believe that a child's forgiveness doesn't count and perhaps the overwhelming importance he had attributed to the accident was due to such a blunder.

His cousin said, "I've been your ambassador for these two months. Bernardo here and Bernardo there. What a relief to hear from Silvia that you're not perfect!"

He looked at him in surprise, because it was the first time he had perceived a tone of rancor in his cousin.

"I'm sorry that you felt that way." And seeing that Josué's glass was empty, he stood up. "I'll pour you another one." He took his glass and went to the bar to fill it.

"Don't pay any attention to me," Josué said.

"No, you're right, I abandoned you a little, but I promise that we'll be together like when you first got here." He handed him the glass of whiskey.

"Don't be so hard on yourself. You've introduced me to all your friends and thanks to that I've had a wonderful time these past two months."

"No, I've taken advantage of you to distance myself from everyone. Every now and then I need to take time off, cut all ties, and you came at the perfect moment."

"You had to deal with that audit."

He looked at his cousin and took a swig of his whiskey.

"There was no audit," he said. Silence, and the first drops of rain sounded against the glass. "I lied to you." He stood up to pour himself another whiskey and sat back down. Josué stared at the rug and the silence lengthened, while outside the rain increased in intensity.

"That's why you invited me to Mexico? So you could sever your ties?" he asked his cousin.

"No, Josué. Your mother's death made me really sad. I loved her very much. That's why I wanted to see you. And your company has filled me with joy. And seeing how well you got along with my friends, I was able to take a break from them, thanks to you."

"Because I was your substitute," Josué said.

"Yes, in a way."

"That's how I felt last night with Lucero. I felt like she was looking at me not as Josué but as Bernardo's cousin. Like a bad copy of you. Did you know that she was in love with you?"

"No, I didn't know. When?"

"When you were with Silvia and went to her house every day. She told me that you never noticed. Silvia doesn't know either. I feel like everyone has looked at me the way she looked at me last night."

"Is that why you want to leave?"

Josué didn't answer and looked back down at the rug. Bernardo stood up with the desire to hug him, but he stopped himself, because he was afraid of being rejected. He went to the window and looked out at the rain.

Josué got up, stood beside him at the window, and, taking a swig of his whiskey, said, "Maybe I came to pay off a debt I owe you."

"What debt?"

"A dirty trick I played on you as a child. It's one of the few memories I have of you."

"What was it?"

"You probably don't remember. We were playing on the balcony of my house, I would run to catch you and you had to escape. I couldn't grab you because you moved so fast, even though you were kneeling. Don't you remember?"

"No, I don't remember. Go on," he said, trying to hide his anxiety.

"You tricked me once again, pretending you were going one way; you went the other way and I followed you straight into the balcony railing. I grabbed the railing and burst into tears. My mother came out to see what was going on, she saw that my face was against the bars of the railing and thought that I had hurt myself, asked me where, and I pointed to my head. I was furious with you, I was crying as if I had actually crashed into the railing, and maybe I even believed I had. My mother took me to my room and rubbed alcohol on my forehead. Then you came in and I still remember your face. You were devastated, afraid to touch me. I realized that I had tricked both of you, and when you left I didn't have the courage to tell my mother the truth. It was my first big lie. I was jealous of you, and that was my way of getting revenge."

"Jealous of me?"

"What's so strange about that? Children at that age are jealous of their younger siblings, so why shouldn't they be jealous of their older cousins? My mother adored you."

He wondered if Josué also felt like a bad copy of him in the eyes of his mother.

"You never told your mother?" he asked.

"No."

He stared at his cousin.

"Why are you looking at me like that?" Josué asked.

"Your scar." And he pointed at his forehead.

Josué raised a hand to his forehead, searching for the scar that he had pointed out to him in the car the day he arrived. He touched it with his finger and said "I remember everything, Josué. I moved out of the way on purpose. That scar is from the injury you got that day."

"You moved?"

"Yes."

"You mean, I really hit my head?"

"Yes."

"Are you sure?"

"I'm not sure of anything anymore. Are you? Are you sure things happened the way you told me?"

"No, it was too long ago."

"Then we'll never know what happened."

"But why did you move?"

"Because I was jealous."

"Jealous of me?" Josué said.

"What's so strange about that? Kids are jealous of their younger brothers and sisters, so why shouldn't they be jealous of their younger cousins? I adored your mother." And after so many years he seemed to understand why his aunt, when she went out to the balcony to see what had happened, didn't ask him anything, didn't reproach him in the slightest, didn't even look him in the eye, and a few months later she moved out of the city with her son.

the next stop

There's nothing worse than an extraordinary story coming out of the mouth of a mediocre narrator, and that was Eduviges, Señor Ramiro's assistant, who came to fix my water heater because Señor Ramiro was sick. While he struggled with the igniting mechanism, he told me about his boss's trip to London the previous summer. "Tell" is one way of putting it, because he interrupted himself off and on to explain something about the thermostat and the boiler's temperature-regulating device, and I was on the verge of giving up completely several times, pretending to pay attention, but then he'd relay some episode or make a comment that pulled me into the story again, and I, irritated with him and with myself, would ask about some detail I hadn't understood.

From his story's confusing collection of fragments, I was able to conclude that Señor Ramiro had borrowed money from friends and relatives to buy a plane ticket to London. His wife's funeral expenses—she'd died a few months before—had left him without savings, and part of the reason for traveling to London to look for his daughter, Esperanza, was to give her the news of her mother's death. He hadn't seen her for three years, and during the previous year he hadn't heard any news from her at all, so it seemed that the parents' relationship with their daughter had never been great. That, at least, was what I deduced from Eduviges's rambling discourse. Esperanza had studied English with a fastidious perfectionism, her sights set on leaving Mexico and her home, where she felt suffocated by an overbearing father and perpetually ill mother.

Lacking the most basic knowledge of the English language, Señor Ramiro stayed in one of the many small hotels in the immediate vicinity of King's

Cross train station, where now and then he'd count his money, because it was the first time he had handled foreign currency. He was suspicious of everything and everyone. He had been misinformed that London was cold; in July it was hotter than Mexico City. He'd bought a wool-lined leather jacket for the trip, and because he was afraid it would be stolen if he left it in his hotel, he wore it everywhere he went. In the parks he saw that the British sat on the grass, but he always chose a bench, and there, at noon, he'd take two cheese sandwiches out of his plastic bag embossed with the crest of the Atlante Soccer Club, the only lunch he ate, and even then he didn't take off his jacket.

The Mexican embassy provided him with the only information they had about his daughter: She had been hired two years earlier as a cleaning supervisor for the TFL, the city's public transportation system. They discovered, however, that the name Esperanza Gutiérrez did not appear on the company's payroll, indicating that she was no longer working there, and they advised him to go in person to the various TFL agencies scattered across the metropolitan area. He was given a list of all of them, and they gave him a map of London and an Oyster card, which he could use to ride the buses and the Tube, and they told him how to use it. He opted to walk from one agency to another, so I suppose that was how he thought of his short stay in London: a long walk in search of his daughter. I can see him wearing his wool-lined jacket, indifferent to the heat, not allowing himself the slightest comfort, as if that would mean some concession that the city could later charge him for, and, for the same reason, perhaps he didn't cry when he finally found the TFL office where Esperanza had worked, first as a cleaning supervisor and then as a receptionist, and he learned that she had died the year before, run over when crossing the street. I don't know how he was given the news, in which language they told him, if they brought him a chair or gave him a glass of water, and if he understood what had happened right away or if they had to explain it to him several times. When I asked Eduviges about those things, he didn't know how to answer me. I assumed the story was over, uttered a few words to express my condolences for that unfortunate outcome, and was about to leave the kitchen when he said, "Subsequently, the next day, a guy went to his hotel looking for him." I turned around, because Eduviges had not, to that point, used the word "subsequently," and that little narrative sparkle stopped me in my tracks. "What guy?" I asked, but he, instead of answering me, asked if I had a Phillips screwdriver because he'd forgotten to bring his. I went to find the screwdriver, gave it to him, and, unable to hide the interest his phrase had awakened in me, asked again, "What guy went looking for him?" He took his time to answer: "You see, he was one of Esperanza's colleagues." He gave the screwdriver a few turns until he removed the screw, appraised the thread, and after informing me that it had to be replaced, threw it into the trash can and asked me, "Where was I?" I refused to answer, and he must have realized that he wasn't being funny because he said, "Ah, right! One of his daughter's colleagues went to his hotel to see him, as I told you." But he got distracted again showing me a screw that he'd pulled out of his toolbox, identical to the one he'd just thrown away. "It's the last one this size I have," he said, and I loathed him, and I realized that it is possible to hate someone for not knowing how to tell a story properly. We exchanged a look draped with the mutual dislike that had fallen between us. Finally, he picked up the thread again and told me that the colleague of Señor Ramiro's daughter didn't speak Spanish, so the communication between the two was arduous. He put it that way, "arduous," showing me that his lexicon wasn't so rickety. The man explained to Señor Ramiro that the TFL office wasn't obliged to pay for his daughter's funeral, so

they had cremated her, and her ashes had gone to
one of the city's municipal cemeteries, the address of
which he brought with him. But that wasn't the only
reason he'd gone to look for him; he also wanted
to let him know that he could hear his daughter's
voice on most of the buses in London. Eduviges
fell silent at that point and patted his vest pockets,
as if looking for something he'd dropped. He was
being ornery again, seeing that I was hanging on
his every word. I asked as calmly as I could what
he meant by "he could hear his daughter's voice on
most of the buses in London." In response he asked
if I had ever been to that city. I told him I had. "And
did you ride a bus?" I answered in the affirma-
tive. Then I understood. I remembered a woman's
voice announcing the names of each bus stop, along
with the final destination. You could hear a message like this: "This is a number five bus to King's
Cross. The next stop: Euston." I connected the dots.
Señor Ramiro's daughter had worked in one of the
TFL offices. The voice that could be heard on some
bus routes was hers. She probably had a beautiful
voice, tinged with a soft Latino accent, and that's
why they'd chosen her to record the names of the
stops. Esperanza's colleague asked Señor Ramiro
to leave the hotel with him, and they walked to the
nearest bus stop together, Eduviges explained. I

imagined the two of them sitting together on the upper deck of the bus. As soon as they heard the recorded voice announcing the next stop, the man must have pointed at the speakers in the ceiling for Señor Ramiro, exclaiming, "Her voice, her voice! Your *hija*! *Escuchar*, it's your *hija*'s voice!"

How long did it take Señor Ramiro to recognize her? Immediately, or did he need to hear it several times to be certain? It would have been futile to ask Eduviges, because that's the kind of detail a bad narrator overlooks. And I wonder how Señor Ramiro reacted when he no longer had the slightest doubt that it was Esperanza's voice. I don't think he felt gratitude, or astonishment, or joy; instead, acute pain. I see him squeezing the top of the seat in front of him so he won't break down and cry, asking himself if that's why he'd come to London, to listen to his dead daughter pronounce the names of the bus stops of that incomprehensible city.

He rode the buses every day, all day, Eduviges told me. He always chose the upper deck, where it was easier to find an empty seat. Not satisfied with hearing his daughter's voice on only one route, he began to listen for it on others. He wound up wanting to hear all the names of the bus stops recorded in her voice, Eduviges said in the only narrative ostentation I heard him use that afternoon. "And did he learn any?" I asked. "He could have learned all of them," he answered, and explained that he rode each route from the first to the last station stop, and if he boarded a bus on a new route and the female voice was not Esperanza's, he got off right away. Then I asked how he paid for all those bus trips, and he replied that he was a fare-beater. But I remembered that transportation inspectors boarded London buses from time to time, and I told him so. "Word of what happened had spread and they left him alone," he said without looking at me.

I looked at him skeptically. London is huge, and no matter how much Señor Ramiro spent his days riding buses and taking different routes, it was almost impossible that all the drivers and inspectors had heard about him. But I thought of his wool-lined jacket, which he took off only when he went to sleep in his hotel, and I imagined that the story of the Mexican plumber who rode buses to hear the voice of his dead daughter could very well have traveled from mouth to mouth among the various TFL offices, even reaching the ears of the transportation inspectors, who turned a blind eye when they recognized his unusual leather jacket. Who would have dared ask him to get off the bus? It was one of those eccentric stories that fascinate the English and that can only happen in London.

I was hardly listening to Eduviges now, who once again had interrupted his story to explain who knows what about the pilot light on the boiler, and while he was talking, I imagined Señor Ramiro living in London for the rest of his life, exploring the length and breadth of it from the top deck of its buses, seized by that voice that now, his wife dead, was all he had left in the world. I saw him wearing a windbreaker someone had given him, more appropriate for London winters than his heavy wool-lined leather jacket. He had learned some English and he got by doing odd plumbing and painting jobs, mainly for the Mexican embassy and some Mexicans residing in London; he knew all the bus routes and had traveled around London more than anyone, but between him and the city there was always the top deck of the buses, with that litany of names that he'd possibly sworn to learn by heart for the eternal salvation of his daughter's soul. And he would have done so, were it not for the fact that one morning, perhaps at the beginning of spring, taking his first bus of the day, he heard the name of the next stop and felt something like a dagger pierce his chest. It wasn't Esperanza's voice. It was lower and more guttural, perhaps a Black woman's, another "beautiful foreign voice." He got to his feet and hurried down the stairs, proceeded to the driver's area, but when he arrived he didn't know what to say and stood there speechless. His English was too elementary to express his surprise or make a complaint. He'd managed to remain silent the whole time he'd been in London, awaiting his daughter's voice and blocking out all the other voices around him.

"All set!" Eduviges said, pulling me out of my reverie, and he showed me the water heater's ignition-mechanism wheel, which had gotten stuck and was now working again. I asked him how much I owed him, he told me the price, I went for the money, paid him, and walked him to the door.

Elena and the children wouldn't be back from my mother-in-law's house for another day, and I kept walking around my house, unable to get Eduviges's story out of my head. I repeated "This is a number five bus to King's Cross. The next stop: Euston" out loud several times, like someone uttering a magic spell. Perhaps the very mediocrity of the narrator had benefited the story, compelling me to take control of its shortcomings to complete it in my own way. Was Esperanza's voice still heard in the famous red double-decker buses or, as I had guessed, had it been replaced by another, since everything changes in this world, even the voice that announces the names of the bus stops in London?

The ignition-mechanism wheel got stuck again two weeks later, something that didn't surprise me after observing that Eduviges the plumber was just as careless as Eduviges the storyteller. I called Señor Ramiro's shop, determined not to pay one penny more for that botched repair. Señor Ramiro answered, I told him why I was calling, and he exclaimed, "That kid's given me nothing but headaches. I'll be right over."

I would have preferred to have Eduviges come back, even though I didn't like him, and I was nervous when I opened the door for Señor Ramiro. He didn't look old or beaten down; he was carrying his enormous toolbox, and since he's familiar with my house, he went straight to the kitchen, where the hot water heater is.

He turned the ignition-mechanism wheel a couple of times and said without looking at me, "I had to fire him. That kid lives on the moon."

He removed the wheel and put two tiny screws in my hand. "Hold these a minute, please, this won't take long."

While he put the mechanism back together he started to whistle.

"You seem happy," I ventured to say.

"As of yesterday, I'm a grandfather," he replied smiling. "My daughter, Esperanza, had a beautiful baby girl."

I thought I misheard him and I cleared my throat. "Your daughter, the one who lives in London?"

"The only one I have. She came back when she found out she was pregnant because she wanted the girl to be born in Mexico."

I looked for some sign of crazy in his eyes. I let a few seconds pass and said, "Eduviges told me that you went to London to...visit her." (I was going to say "look for" but I stopped myself in time.)

He turned to me and said with a look of pity, "I tell you, there's something wrong with that kid's head! I've never left Mexico in my life...Now, if you could, give me those two screws, please."